Bluegrass Series

Bluegrass State of Mind

Risky Shot

Dead Heat

Bluegrass Brothers

Bluegrass Undercover

Rising Storm

Secret Santa: A Bluegrass Series Novella

Acquiring Trouble

Relentless Pursuit

Secrets Collide

Final Vow

Bluegrass Singles

All Hung Up

Bluegrass Dawn

The Perfect Gift

The Keeneston Roses

Forever Bluegrass Series

Forever Entangled

Forever Hidden

Forever Betrayed

Forever Driven

Forever Secret

Forever Surprised

Forever Concealed

Forever Devoted

Forever Hunted

Forever Guarded

Forever Notorious

Forever Ventured (coming later in 2019)

<u>Shadows Landing Series</u>

Saving Shadows

Sunken Shadows (coming May 14, 2019)

Lasting Shadows (coming later in 2019)

<u>Women of Power Series</u>

Chosen for Power

Built for Power

Fashioned for Power

Destined for Power

<u>Web of Lies Series</u>

Whispered Lies

Rogue Lies

Shattered Lies

<u>Moonshine Hollow Series</u>

Moonshine & Murder

Moonshine & Malice (coming March 26, 2019)

Moonshine & Mayhem (coming April 16, 2019)

PROLOGUE

ZOEY MATHERS WAS JUST ABOUT to leave her law office in the most prestigious skyscraper in downtown Los Angeles. At twenty-eight, she was working her way up the ladder at the entertainment firm with her eye on the senior associate position. And today had been a good day.

Zoey turned off the lamp in her cubicle and walked down the dark halls. It was almost two in the morning and she was going home to celebrate her big deal—all thanks to Scott Westerfield. Scott was her star client. He was the next big Hollywood action hero, and he'd picked her to negotiate the deal for his next action movie franchise. She'd just gotten the last signatures needed on the thirty-million-dollar contract and had sent it to Scott and his agent. Her boss had been thrilled. The words "junior" and "partner" were being spoken with her name attached to them. There was a chance she'd skip straight to partner, and she was so excited she did a little dance in the elevator.

It had been a little tenuous to get the deal to go through. Scott had only selected her because when he'd walked by her toward the conference room she'd been bending over the filing cabinet, and he thought she had a nice butt. Hey, she'd take any in she could if it got her off her current ninety-hour workweeks. Even if that meant putting up with his constant talk about sex, drugs, parties, and all the things he shouldn't be doing if he wanted to stay employed.

Zoey hit the elevator button as her phone rang. SCOTT WESTERFIELD showed up. "No, no, no. Please don't be anything bad," Zoey said as she answered the phone. "Scott?"

"Dude," he whispered into the phone. "You have to save me. I'm surrounded by shiny goblins trying to kill me!"

"What?" Zoey asked with dread as she pushed the button to the parking garage.

"Freaking goblins! They're slithering all over me."

"Are you crying?"

"Save me!"

The image of the movie deal being ripped apart flashed a second before the image of her junior partnership being flushed down the drain.

"Where are you?"

"I'm at the Sparkling Tassel. Oh no, they're coming!" The phone thudded as Scott screamed. The Sparkling Tassel was a strip club all the celebrities went to. Knowing the movie deal had a morals clause in it, Zoey raced from the elevator to her car. She sped through the still-occupied streets of downtown to the strip club to rescue him, the deal, and her career.

When she'd arrived at the brightly colored Sparkling Tassel, the parking lot was packed. Great. There were going to be photos, and she'd need to pay off a lot of people to get them deleted. Zoey slid to a stop and parked her car by the front door before hurrying inside. She slammed her palms against the metallic door covered in fake diamonds and shoved it open.

Zoey was assaulted by the sound of thumping music, laughter, screaming, and the high-pitched wailing of her client. She looked around and was met with the vision of a naked Scott swinging on a stripper pole while crying as all hell was breaking loose on the stage. The escorts he'd brought with him to the club were on the stage, screaming and fighting with the club's strippers, all of whom were in various stages of undress. The escorts' pimp was trying to round them up, but it was like herding wet cats. Men were packed around the stage, shouting encouragements and suggestions.

"The drugs they took were dirty," the deep masculine voice of a mountain of a man said next to her. Zoey looked over at a large muscled arm, then followed it up to the symbol tattooed on his neck. It was a circle of black swords with a red drop of blood in the middle. It matched the black vest over a black T-shirt that stretched tight across his wide chest and thick biceps, black pants, and combat boots.

"Is that pleather?" Zoey asked with a raised eyebrow at the pants and vest that did nothing to hide the sexy man under them.

"Yup. Easy to clean. You just hose it down," the man said as he looked her over. "Armani?"

Zoey looked down at her white pencil skirt and light pink silk blouse and nodded. "Good eye. Why are you just standing here? Shouldn't you be up there stopping them?" Zoey watched as Scott spun around the pole and landed hard on the ground. One of the escorts had another by her weave. With a sickening scream, the weave came off.

The victorious escort held it in her hand, her eyes wide with surprise while the other woman covered her head with her hands. The escort shook the weave off her hand, sending it flying and landing on Scott's shoulder. Scott screamed as if he'd been castrated, flung the weave to the floor, and peed on it.

"Nope. I'll let the cops take this one. They're on the way," the bouncer said. "Now, if they start destroying property, I'll get up there. But this is just amusement for everyone."

Zoey's stomach plummeted. No, no, no! "Did you say cops?"

"Yeah. They'll be here any minute. So, are you his wife?" he asked as he nodded to Scott.

"No, I'm his attorney. Do you have a backdoor to this place?"

"Of course we do," he said with a nod of his head to a back hallway that looked as if it led to the gates of hell. It was dark as the lights barely gave off a yellow tinted glow that somehow didn't illuminate anything. When Zoey squinted, she would have sworn something was moving back there.

"Ugh!" Zoey was forced to do what any good entertainment lawyer did—especially one who wanted to save her potential promotion. Zoey pushed away from the safety of the door and hurried to the stage. She had to skirt tables and push through the men lining the stage who were whooping and hollering as Zoey stepped up on a chair, hiked up her skirt, and climbed onto the shiny black stage. The men's hollers grew louder, and the escorts and strippers turned to see what the noise was all about. That's when things went from bad to worse.

By the time the cops arrived, Zoey had a hunk of her long reddish-brown hair torn out and tossed on the stage, which her client had peed on, a slit torn up her skirt, her blouse ripped partially off of her, and somehow she only had one shoe.

"Hands behind your back," the cop standing in front of her said as he pulled a pair of cuffs out.

Panic like none other filled her. She couldn't be arrested! "But I'm a lawyer!"

"Look lady, half the women up here are in law school or medical school. Hands now."

"No, you don't get it. I'm trying to stop the fight."

"That'll teach you to keep your hands off my man!" the woman who'd ripped Zoey's shirt yelled as she was dragged away in handcuffs. "Just because you charge more doesn't mean you get my man!"

"No, I'm . . ." Zoey had started to argue when the cuffs were closed over her hands and the police officer hauled her from the stage.

"Zoey," Scott called out. "I'll pay your bill when I get out of jail. Thanks again for today. Hey!" Scott yelled, "Why isn't anyone arresting that unicorn? He's pooping rainbows on the sidewalk."

That son of a . . . The door to the cruiser hadn't even closed before the door to her career slammed shut. News and gossip outlets were already playing video of them being escorted out of the strip club by the police and someone had managed to snap a couple pictures inside. She saw herself on the television in the booking room— up on the stage, fighting with one of the strippers as Scott sat crying.

"In you go," the officer said after she'd been booked.

Her call to her office went unanswered. Similarly, her calls to all of her lawyer friends were too. Desperation and panic filled her unlike any she'd ever felt before. Everything she had worked for, all the years in school, all the time studying, the long hours working—it was over. She knew it.

Zoey hung up the phone and the woman officer who was letting her use the phone looked sympathetically at her before putting her back into the holding cell.

The minutes were excruciatingly slow as they ticked by while Zoey tried to figure out who to call to bail her out.

"Zoey Mathers," an officer called out as she stepped to the bars an hour later. "You've made bail."

"Who bailed me out?" Zoey asked with a mixture of relief and trepidation at facing whoever it was in the waiting room.

"Don't know, but he's good-looking. A word of advice," she said as she handed Zoey her things back. "Try to find another way to pay off law school."

Zoey was about to protest she wasn't an escort when the door to the waiting room opened and there stood the man in black pleather.

"You?"

"You," he said back with a slow grin.

"What? Why?" she asked as if she couldn't gather any more words.

The man cupped her elbow and led her from the police station. "I thought you could use a helping hand tonight," he said, shoving a bike helmet into her hands.

He put on his own helmet and swung one pleather-encased leg over his motorcycle. "Come on, sweetness. Let me take you home."

"Are you going to hack me up into a hundred pieces and leave parts of my body all around LA?"

She didn't hear him laugh, but saw his shoulders moving as he shook his head. "No. It just feels like the right thing to do. Come on. I got your address when I bailed you out."

"Where's my shoe?"

"Starr Bright took it home. Apparently even just one of those shoes can get her a hundred bucks."

Maybe being killed wouldn't be so bad. At least she wouldn't have to face her boss in the morning. Zoey took a deep breath and climbed onto the motorcycle with one foot wearing a high heel and the other bare. She clung to his thick strong body from her seat on the back of his motorcycle as he navigated his way to her condo in the hottest part of LA.

"Thank you for bailing me out. If you give me your address I'll mail you a check for the money you had to put up."

"It's okay. I know you're good for it," he said as he turned off his bike and removed his helmet.

"You don't have to come up," Zoey said as she set her helmet on the seat.

He didn't answer, instead just cupped her elbow again and walked her inside. She smiled tightly at the night guard as they made their way to the elevator and then up to her floor without saying a word. When the elevator doors opened, Zoey paused.

"Are you sure you're not going to murder me?"

"I hardly would have come to your video-monitored condo to do so. You're safe with me, sweetness."

Zoey stepped from the elevator, turned down the hall, and stopped in her tracks. Three boxes sat by her door. He bent down and picked them up, along with the note notifying her of her termination from the law firm. Tears pressed against the back of her eyes as he quietly moved about her home as if he had been there before. He directed her to the couch, brought a glass from the kitchen and filled it with vodka before handing it to her.

"Drink," he ordered.

"I've been fired," she said numbly as she looked at all her possessions from work along with her notice of termination.

"So, you'll get another job."

"What's your name?" Zoey finally asked. She didn't even realize she didn't know who he was.

"Slade."

"Slade what?"

"Just Slade."

Zoey tossed back the drink and Slade refilled it. She needed the pain to stop. "Well, Just Slade, California may be a big state, but there's no outrunning this. I'm a national joke now. There's nowhere I can practice law that I won't be recognized. My career is over. My *life* is over." She tossed back the second drink and started to feel better. The hysterical panic pressing on her started to relax with the warmth of the liquor. Oh crap, her life was over. The panic rose again.

Slade handed her the third drink and sat down next to her on a couch that cost her almost ten thousand dollars and suddenly looked small and about to break with a man as large as Slade sitting on it. "Did you always want to be an attorney?"

Zoey started to feel fuzzy. Her body began to relax, but she was still so worried she thought she might throw up. "No. When I was a kid I wanted to be a baker." And that's when the idea struck her. "That's what I'll do. I'll go someplace new. I'll start over. Give it a couple years and I'll slowly get back into law someplace new after the scandal dies down. Maybe change my name too." Hope filled her, or maybe it was just the alcohol.

"Where will you go?" Slade asked, his long legs spread out before him as he slung his arm along the back of the couch.

"I don't know. I'm a California girl. My father died when I was young, and my mom's second husband is a plastic surgeon to the stars, so she's never lived anywhere else either." Zoey sighed. Her own mother hadn't answered her call. She'd been at some charity ball or dinner party or who knows what. Whatever it was, it was more important than her daughter. Zoey closed her eyes against the pain of their estrangement and focused on the future. "It's kind of overwhelming when you think about it. How can I possibly choose someplace to live?"

Slade lifted his hips and pulled out a knife. Zoey shrank back into her couch remembering what he said about how easy pleather was to clean. She'd been top in her class at law school, yet here she was with an armed stranger in her apartment. What had she been thinking? Well, she hadn't been. She'd been too consumed by fear and self-pity to think about making good decisions. "You said you wouldn't murder me."

Slade shook his head. "This is Lady Luck. Do you have a map of the United States?"

"Who uses maps? It's all online now," Zoey said reaching for her phone.

Slade shook his head. "Fine. Give me your laptop."

Ten minutes later, a collage of printouts was taped on the wall. She had her map. The entire country laid out in front of her. "Come here," Slade said, pulling her from the couch and tying a dishtowel around her eyes as a blindfold. Zoey couldn't see as he spun her around, moved her right and left, and then placed the hilt of the knife in her hand. "Walk until the knife sticks in the wall. Where it lands is where you will land. Fate will guide you to where you should be."

1

THREE MONTHS LATER...

IT HAD TAKEN Zoey eight days to pack up her stuff, get the charges dropped, and drive across the country to Moonshine Hollow, Tennessee. She had sold her couch in LA and used the money to rent a small shop on Main Street in Moonshine for a year. It had taken her three weeks to clean the place and get it set up as a bakery. It was a small space, but it was *her* space. Pride filled her as she looked around. There was a glass door with a pink bell over it that chimed every time it was opened. A large plate glass window took up the remainder of the front wall. She had put up a pink and white awning with Zoey's Sweet Treats written in black script. Inside, she had five bistro tables set up in the open space before the refrigerated case that formed a wall between the sitting area and the kitchens. Behind the refrigerated case was room to move around and stock the cases before a set of swinging door led to the kitchen area. To the far right of the cases was a cash register and an opening to get into the front of the shop.

For the three weeks it had taken Zoey set up her shop, she had lived in the small studio apartment upstairs until she knew how much money she would have left to find a place to live. She hadn't needed to worry. Her apartment in LA sold after two weeks. Three days after she opened Zoey's Sweet Treats, a check arrived from her realtor. Zoey also sold her flashy sports car in LA and drove the rented moving van to Moonshine Hollow, leaving her to look for a place near downtown that wouldn't require a car. She found her house only three blocks away from her bakery and was able to buy it with the money from the sale of her condo and car. It was a cute cottage house painted blue, more of a nautical blue than navy, and trimmed with white. There was a small porch with a wooden swing, all painted white, and flowers lining the short brick walkway from the street to her porch. The view from her porch was lovely and the view from her back patio was breathtaking.

Moonshine Hollow was a small town of under a thousand people. Most had lived there since their ancestors climbed the mountains, following explorers who had pushed the American frontier farther west. The town was settled when the pioneers found the small meadow with a mountain stream running next to it, nestled between the Appalachian Mountains. Originally it had been Earnest Creek, named after Ned Earnest who had been the leader of the group of ragtag settlers who founded the area in the late seventeen hundreds. It stayed Earnest Creek until 1920 and Prohibition. The residents of Earnest Creek put out the finest moonshine in the country. People traveled all over looking for that "Holler where the moonshine is made." Earnest Creek became known as Moonshine Hollow, and in a town meeting for the history books, the town outvoted the Earnest family and changed the name to Moonshine Hollow.

As a new homeowner and resident of Moonshine Hollow, Zoey spent her evenings on her back patio, staring at the mountains and watching the waters of Earnest Creek while recipes came to her—like the Chocolate Temptation she just finished making in the bakery. Zoey moaned with the pleasure of smooth chocolate melting in her mouth as the pink bell tinkled, indicating someone had opened the front door.

She set down the chocolate torte to see who it was. She'd received a mixed reception when she'd arrived in town three months earlier. The town was used to people leaving, not arriving. At first they'd walked by the shop and stared through the large window while they whispered to each other. But when Zoey had finally opened two months ago, there hadn't been a shortage of people coming in for a free sample. Ever since then, she'd had a steady flow of customers. Enough that she was no longer reaching into her savings account to pay for groceries, and enough to keep her busy so that LA was just a distant memory, even though she still received notifications of her name popping up in legal magazines every now and then.

"I told you she's baking up something new." Zoey heard the old twangy voice and immediately knew who was there. She smiled at the pleasure of having found people like Vilma and Agnes. Who knew she'd find a family all the away across the country? But the two old women had become just that.

Zoey grabbed a tray of cupcakes and carried them out front. "Hi Vilma. Hi Agnes." Zoey smiled to the two old sisters who had adopted her since her arrival. They lived a few houses down the road from her and had brought her a basket full of muffins they swore would give her energy to clean. Sure enough they had. Since then, they saw each other practically every day and Zoey considered them family. In those short months, they were more loving, supportive, and kind than her own mother had ever been.

"What did you make today?" Agnes asked as she sat down and patted her tight steel gray curls. The women must have just come from the hair salon down the street. There wasn't much on Main Street, but it was the only place to go in Moonshine if you needed something. There was a salon, a small grocery, a hardware store, a clothing boutique, a bank, the courthouse, the only lawyer's office, a small diner, and a large hunting equipment store. It was the South after all.

"I told you, it's gonna be something special," Vilma said as she rubbed her wrinkled hands together. Her white hair was in similarly permed-within-an-inch-of-its-life curls. The two sisters were of an undetermined age somewhere between old and ancient and always wore complementing tracksuits. Today Vilma was in a pale yellow velour suit while Agnes wore a pale blue one.

Zoey smiled and held up her finger to indicate they should wait. A second later Zoey brought a slice of the torte and three forks to the bistro table they were sitting at. "I call it Chocolate Temptation."

The sisters oohed and dove in. "Oh my Goddess, um *goodness*, this is amazing," Agnes moaned.

"This is pure magic," Vilma sighed.

"I take it you think I should add it to my menu?" Zoey smiled as she wiped her hands on her apron and picked up the fork to take a bite. The pleasure Zoey got from seeing her creations enjoyed eclipsed the pleasure she'd felt when she'd negotiated a multimillion dollar deal. She never would have guessed she could feel so fulfilled when she'd left her old life behind.

"It would be a sin to not make it every day," Agnes said before taking another bite and closing her eyes.

Zoey laughed and picked up the empty plate. Something in her soul had found peace in Moonshine. Agnes and Vilma were a large part of the reason why, along with the other friends she'd made. Her body knew what to do when it was time to bake. Zoey couldn't understand it, but Agnes and Vilma said they did. They'd spent hours sitting outside watching the creek, eating Zoey's creations, and talking about life. She'd found something that had eluded her, despite all of her previous success. She'd found happiness.

2

ZOEY CLOSED the box of the last batch of desserts to be delivered and stacked the boxes into her large pink and white polka dot canvas wagon with Zoey's Sweet Treats written across the side. She had three deliveries to make tonight before the town's gathering at Earnest Park to pick the newest Moonshine of the Year flavor.

The famous distillery started all those centuries ago by Ned Earnest was still going strong and was the bulk of the town's economy. Nearly everyone either worked for or had retired from the distillery. Because of that, the citizens of the town were more than simply residents—they were lifelong friends. It had taken Zoey months, but finally she was no longer looked at with suspicion. However, she wasn't quite one of them yet. Zoey accepted that as she packed her wagon. The baking helped keep her mind off such things. And while she may not have been born and bred in Moonshine Hollow, she was slowly becoming accepted. People had even begun to share all the latest gossip with her when they came into her bakery. That made Zoey feel like she belonged. Nothing brought people together like gossip.

Zoey pulled her wagon out of the store and locked the glass door. Her first stop was two doors down at the Lodge of the Order of the Opossum. Zoey stopped at the thick wooden door and knocked. The eye-height six-inch wooden panel slid open and a pair of old brown eyes narrowed at her.

"What's the password?" he demanded.

Zoey rolled her eyes. "Bart, do I have to do this every week?"

"No one can enter without the password," Bart told her as he slammed the panel closed.

Every. Freaking. Week. Zoey knocked on the door again and Bart slid open the small panel. "Password."

Zoey let out a sigh. "Oh great opossum, I beg entrance into this hallowed lodge to deliver the sustenance for your passel. The password is *jacks*," Zoey said the word referring to male opossums.

Bart looked down at her wagon, "You brought those opossum cookies for us?"

"Yes, Bart," Zoey said as she smiled. She brought the cookies every week. They were sugar cookies decorated to look like opossum. After her first week in business, she'd been contracted to bring them every week. They'd been her first big client.

The bolt to the door opened and Bart stepped back to let her into the sacred lodge. The lodge consisted of a bar and a large television hooked up to a satellite dish. The opossums were a group of old married men who simply wanted to watch sports and drink in peace. Women were strictly prohibited from the lodge, but they made an exception for Zoey for the simple reason they didn't know how to cook and depended on her for snacks. Every week Zoey brought them cookies and was immediately caught up on the town's gossip.

"Hey Zoey," Billy Ray called out from behind the bar. None of the opossums were younger than fifty. They called any married man who hadn't been married for thirty years a newlywed. Once you'd been married for thirty years, you could join the Order of the Opossums.

"Evening, Billy Ray," Zoey called out, and she pulled her wagon to the bar. Billy Ray was sixty-five and had a gray beard that would impress lumberjacks. He said he hadn't trimmed it in five years, ever since he wife told him to cut that nasty thing off his face.

"Did you hear? Peach kicked Otis out of the house last night."

Zoey looked to where Otis stood, leaning on his cane and guzzling a beer as he was being timed by a couple of the men. "He looks heartbroken."

"Heck, no. He's been married forty-eight years. He's having the time of his life. We figure Peach will call him home in a couple days when the yard needs to be mowed. Until then, he's living it up."

Zoey handed over the boxes of cookies and Billy Ray slid her an envelope in cash. Zoey had gotten a credit card scanner, but no one in Moonshine used credit cards. The IRS could track them, and the IRS was more feared than Satan himself.

Zoey waved goodbye to the group of men and headed to the building across the street. The large front window had stained glass in the image of a purple iris. A wooden door was similarly painted with a field of irises. Zoey knocked on the door, and it cracked open on a security chain.

"Password," a little old lady said pleasantly.

"Hello, Peach. I heard about Otis," Zoey said with a grin as she looked at Peach, semi-hidden behind the door.

"Ugh. Don't remind me. I worked for three weeks to get him to leave and finally gave up and kicked him out when he said my meatloaf was a bit dry. As if. And it's been blissful without him there this week. I've cleaned out his closet, had the house painted by that young Justin Merkle, and ate at the club every night. It's been heaven. Now, what's the password so we can get a bite of this new dessert Vilma was telling us about."

Zoey let out a long suffering breath. She wasn't a member of the Opossums and she wasn't a member the women's counterpart, the Irises, but she was required to comply with their secret traditions anyway just to enter their clubs to drop off her deliveries.

"Men are stupid, bless their hearts."

Peach closed the door and the chain slid free before the door opened wide. Peach's hair was dyed honey yellow and worn in a cute chin-length bob, presently pulled back from her face by an old fashioned decorative comb. As Zoey stepped inside, she almost laughed at the differences between the Irises and the Opossums. The Opossums' den was dark and dirty with wood floors, wood walls, wood bar, and old torn furniture. The Irises lived in light and beauty. Their couches were fresh and clean with bright floral patterns. The walls were painted a light purple, the bathroom a fresh green, and there was a full kitchen that would make any chef envious.

The Irises also had satellite television, but it was mostly on The Hallmark Channel. Once a month, they would buy a pay-per-view event of The Thunder From Down Under or some Vegas show that involved scantily clad men.

"Good evening, Zoey!" The heads of white, gray, and dyed hair called out from their places on the couches around the room.

"Evenin' sugar. Are you excited to vote for the new flavor of moonshine for this year?" Fay asked as she got up to help with the food. Fay was tall and thin with a hairstyle that looked as if it hadn't changed since the 1950s. She was every bit Southern from the tip of her perfectly manicured hands that could outshoot most of the men to her pedicured toes that had grown up hiking these woods and dancing the jig.

"I am. I've heard the rumors that the Opossums came up with a new flavor." Zoey wanted the scoop. Every year the Opossums, the Irises, and the Mountaineers, the other club in town, all developed a different flavor. The town would vote on their favorite and the Moonshine Distillery would manufacture the winner as a limited edition special for one year.

"Ha! Probably Dirty Laundry Moonshine," Peach said sarcastically as she started setting out the tortes and slicing them up.

Fay got up and passed out the plates. Zoey smiled at the collective moan of pleasure as the group tried the first bite. This was way better than winning any mediation. Here, everyone was happy.

"Who needs a husband when we have this?" Peach cried out as the group of white hairs tittered with laughter in agreement.

Zoey said her goodbyes as she was slipped a light purple cash-filled envelope with her name written across it in beautiful script. No one, even the smart and sassy Irises, would pay with a credit card. Zoey stepped outside and took a deep breath. Spring was in the air. The leaves were in full bloom and the night air smelled of new beginnings. She had three boxes of cookies to deliver to the Mountaineers at the other end of Main Street before she could go home and get ready for the big vote that night.

The Mountaineers were completely different from the older groups she had just visited. The Mountaineers were the younger people of Moonshine Hollow. Anyone twenty-one years and older could join. It was a co-ed group filled with young couples full of love and affection, along with single people just wanting a place to hang out. They constantly made fun of their parents in the Irises or the Opossums. Zoey just smiled, knowing in twenty-eight more years these honeymooning couples would be plotting and lying to get away from each other and go to their respective clubs.

Zoey had been appalled at first, but then she realized the couples were actually still very much in love. They just needed some time apart with friends to stay happy. She guessed after thirty years everyone needed a little bit of a break or someone might end up dead with their face in an apple pie and a fork in their back. And by someone, she meant one of the husbands. Bless their hearts.

The Mountaineers didn't hide behind wood doors or stain glass windows. Anyone could look in at them laughing, playing pool, or even making out like the newlyweds some of them were. Their numbers were also smaller than the other groups. Younger people from Moonshine left the hollow in large groups at the age of eighteen. Some went to Knoxville or Nashville to experience the big city and never came home. Some went off to college and never came back. Those who remained were a mix of people went to work at the distillery or a family business in town after high school. Finally there was a smaller number of people who left the town for college or excitement, but came back to their roots.

Sometimes these people brought new spouses back with them. Zoey could spot those newcomers by their constant look of surprise or confusion. She'd had that same look for the first month she was in Moonshine. Zoey had been asked to join their club, but before she could answer the sickeningly happy couples were already trying to set her up, so she'd politely claimed she was too busy setting up her new shop to join just then.

"Zoey!" her new best friend, Maribelle, called out.

Maribelle was dating another member, Dale, and was in the moony-eyed courtship period of their relationship. Her red hair and freckles were adorably cute, which was a word Maribelle hated. It didn't help that she had a young face and was barely five feet two inches tall. Maribelle was Zoey's neighbor. She was twenty-six and had moved back to Moonshine a year ago, after teaching in Chattanooga for a couple years. She was the newest teacher at Moonshine High School, and Zoey adored her. Together they could laugh, tell secrets, and just be young friends trying to figure out their lives.

It seemed like yesterday Maribelle had frantically knocked on Zoey's door for something pretty to wear on her first date with Dale. Dale was Maribelle's complete opposite. Maribelle was talkative, outgoing, short, and full of energy. Dale was six foot four and two hundred sixty pounds of solid muscle. His voice was deep, and he was quiet, but you could tell a lot went on under his neatly trimmed beard and thick brown hair.

"Evening, Maribelle. Are you ready to debut your moonshine flavor tonight?" Zoey asked as she starting stacking the chocolate chip, moonshine frosted, and chocolate peanut butter chip cookies on the folding tables. Where the Opossums' furniture screamed bachelor basics and the Irises' reeked of elegant mom, the Mountaineers' cried poor college students. Their decor consisted of old couches from their parents, folding tables, plastic crates with an old door across it to form a low table, and pillows for people to sit on around the makeshift table. Their bar was full of moonshine, cheap beer, and boxes of wine.

"We are so excited. It's going to be fantastic. Something those old fogies would never think of." Then Maribelle whispered, "And, Dale is taking me tonight."

Zoey followed Maribelle's gaze and smiled in wonder. "That's wonderful. So it's getting serious?" The man wasn't just a Mountaineer, he was the whole freaking mountain. His strong face was hidden under a trimmed light-brown beard. Dale was also a catch. His family had been farming the area for a hundred years. They had a small family farm at the edge of the hollow. They had some crops, but mostly goats that were happy in the mountains.

"Yes, I know I told you last night we were taking it slow. I mean, his parents didn't know until the other day that we were dating. But after meeting his parents, he's been dropping more long-term hints. He even mentioned heading to Nashville for a weekend to see a concert. I'm so excited. And, he has a friend," Maribelle practically vibrated with excitement while Zoey's heart sank.

"Oh, no. Not another blind date. Not after the whole Wayne debacle. The town is still talking about it."

"Well, you did pour a bowl of beef stew over his head at the Moonshine Diner," Maribelle shrugged.

"He called me stupid for not accepting his marriage proposal—twenty minutes after I met him. He said he didn't want to marry a stupid cow and I'll never do better than him. And that was before saying it was really a pity proposal because he felt so bad for me for being a stupid cow. I thought it was nice of me to only dump the stew on him as opposed to the other things I was thinking of doing with the flatware," Zoey defended.

"Well, what's done is done and Wayne is dating Missy now." Maribelle glanced to where Wayne had his thick slimy hand on Missy's ass as he sent Zoey a wink. Ugh!

"No thank you. No more blind dates."

"But Luke Tanner is perfect for you. He's just moved back to Moonshine about a year ago after being hired by the sheriff's department. He was born here, but his parents divorced. He and his mother moved away when he was sixteen. He was a detective in Knoxville and got tired of the big city and moved back here."

Zoey nodded. She'd seen him at a distance. It may be a small town, but she'd been so busy with work she hadn't gotten to know everyone yet. "I think I know who he is. But I told you, no more blind dates!"

"Well, Luke will look for you at the park. Dale said he was looking forward to meeting you." Maribelle winked, totally ignoring Zoey's protest.

Zoey gave her friend a forced smile. "Yay!"

3

The park was packed. On the far side, kids played in the twisting stream as water ran down the mountain and over the smooth rocks through Moonshine Hollow. A large barn with the doors open hosted a bluegrass band and dancing while tents were erected outside where the townsfolk could taste and vote on the new moonshine flavors.

Zoey greeted the people she knew and smiled at those she hadn't yet met as she made her way to the nearest tent. She scanned the area as she waited in line to see if she could find her blind date for the night. Zoey was still torn on whether she would avoid him or introduce herself upon finding him in the crowd.

"Hey Zoey." Zoey turned to see Justin Merkle, a friend of Wayne's, stepping into line behind her. She was trying not to hold that friendship against Justin, but Justin had been standoffish at first. And more recently he had been rubbing her the wrong way. It was obvious Wayne was having an impact on his friend.

"Hi, Justin. Do you think your recipe will win tonight?"

Zoey asked the tall gangly man. He was lean, but he was incredibly strong. He painted houses and did odd jobs around town as a handy man.

"I hope so. It's not up my alley, but it's still really good. Kinda like you are." Justin let his gaze roam up her body and Zoey quickly stepped away.

Zoey stepped up to the table and relaxed as Vilma and Agnes smiled at her. "So, you have a date with Luke Tanner tonight?" Vilma winked as Agnes handed her a paper tray with three small paper cups on it. Each cup had a number on it: 1, 2, or 3. Then there was one poker chip on the tray.

"I would call it more of an ambush than a date. I didn't know anything about it until Maribelle told me an hour ago," Zoey replied.

"Give him a try. He's a good one," Agnes told her as she handed Justin a tray.

"Ugh. Maybe," Zoey said as she was already trying to find all the exits just in case.

"Bat your lashes, you may have some competition," Vilma called out as Zoey walked away. Great. Now she was being set up with a man who may or may not be available. She didn't want competition. She wanted chocolate.

ZOEY STOOD off to the side and tasted the samples. Number one was peach flavored. She guessed it was the Irises' mix. Number two was bacon moonshine—the Opossums. Number three was fresh and light. It was sweet and tart at the same time. There was a hint of cherry in it, and when Zoey cast her vote, she put her poker chip in the box for moonshine number three.

"Zoey Mathers?"

A slow deep voice behind her had her spinning from the voting boxes. A man with light-brown hair, deep gray eyes, and a smooth face with angles that were more sinful than her torte.

"Yes?" Zoey answered as she dragged her eyes from lips she thought were perfect for kissing. He looked nothing like the other men her age in Moonshine. They were more . . . rustic.

"I'm Luke Tanner, your blind date."

He held out his hand and Zoey noticed the badge and gun on his hip.

"Nice to meet you," Zoey said as she shook his hand.

"Nice to meet you too. I'm sorry," he blinked and shook his head. "It's just that when Vilma, Agnes, Maribelle, and Dale talked me into this date they made it sound like a pity date. I wasn't expecting someone normal."

A pity date. Oh, she was going to kill those meddling busy bodies. A pity date! She was stuck on a freaking pity date. Could this night get any worse?

ZOEY JINXED HERSELF. The evening had been a disaster. Luke had been the perfect gentleman even as she plotted her revenge on her friends. Luke was getting used to being back in a small town. He was overrun with casseroles and pies from every woman in town, even though he'd been back in Moonshine Hollow for nine months. He was happy to be away from the death and evil he saw working as a homicide detective in Knoxville.

Luke was polite and funny. He told her stories of growing up in Moonshine and some of the funnier calls that had come into the sheriff's office since his return. But Zoey noticed he mentioned a doctor named Ava from Keeneston, Kentucky quite a bit and figured that was her so-called competition.

Zoey was going to ask about Ava, because it sounded as if they were involved in some way, even if it was just his desire to be involved with her. But before she could ask, it was time for the announcement of the winner of Flavor of the Year.

Miss Moonshine Hollow stood on the stage in her sequined evening gown with her hair piled on top of her head in curls, highlighting her over-the-top-large crown. Tim Hildebrand, the keeper of the distillery's recipes had slowly made his way onto the stage and handed a card to Miss Moonshine Hollow. Miss Moonshine squealed and held up the envelope.

"Ladies and gentlemen, the votes have been counted. The new moonshine flavor of the year is . . ." Miss Moonshine used her long nail to rip the sticker and open the card. "Bacon!"

The men had cheered. The Irises frowned in unison. The Mountaineers shrugged. But then Peach had turned to Otis and stomped her foot.

"You had to take this away from me. Bacon! That was my recipe. I made that for your no good hide back when you were a good and loving husband. How dare you use my own recipe against me?" Peach poked Otis in his chest, and Otis just smirked in return.

That's when Peach lost it and dumped an entire pitcher of sweet tea over his head. Otis stood, looking like a wet chicken, before slowly turning to the table and picking up a key lime pie. Before Zoey knew it, he'd turned that pie upside down on Peach's head. Globs of key lime pie fell onto Peach's shoulders, ears, and even dangled off her nose.

"Aw, no," Luke said as he shook his head. "I'm sorry, Zoey, but I believe our evening is at an end."

Zoey nodded with wide eyes and an open mouth as Fay launched a tray of banana pudding into the group of Opossums. The entire town was silent for a space of three seconds before all hell broke loose. Food was thrown. Drinks were tossed. The entire town parted in half as they chose sides in Peach and Otis's fight. Miss Moonshine shrieked as a spoonful of brownie and whipped cream trifle splattered in her face.

"I meant to walk you home, but I guess I have to cut to the chase. Would you care to have dinner with me this week? I enjoyed talking to you, and I think we could be . . . friends?" Luke asked as he pulled apart a pair of senior citizens battling over control of a peach cobbler.

Zoey smiled at Luke. Even though she had started off the date horribly embarrassed at being the recipient of pity, Luke was a man every woman dreamed of but very few ever had the chance to meet. "I'd like that." She would have to see where it went and who exactly that Ava was. It wasn't likely, but maybe she was his sister.

"Great. I'll pick you up tomorrow. Six thirty sound good? It was real nice spending the evening with you, Zoey." Luke smiled and was hit with a cream pie in the face. His tongue came out and licked the cream off his lips as his fingers cleaned the cream from his eyes. Instead of anger over being pied in the face, Luke tossed back his head and laughed.

His gray eyes twinkled in amusement, and Zoey knew Luke Tanner was someone she wanted to get to know better. He was unlike anyone she had ever met in California.

A CHILL SWEPT over Zoey as she walked home. She rubbed

her bare arms to chase off the goosebumps as she walked through town. If she hadn't known Moonshine Hollow so well and the people in it, she might have been scared. The town appeared abandoned. Main Street was shut down. Store lights were off. She was alone on the street with only the echo of her footsteps to keep her company.

For a moment, she thought she should have waited for Luke to escort her home. But he would be late, trying to break apart the epic food fight, and she had to get up early to bake.

Zoey turned off Main Street onto Stillhouse Lane. Stillhouse Lane ran to the distillery on the outskirts of town. Her street, Runner Road, was the next left. And then she'd finally be home. Her sweet cottage called to her tonight. The peacefulness and the comfort of her little home was so different from her high end modern condo in LA.

The houses on Runner Road all had their interior lights off and their porch lights on as all the residents were at the festival. They would stumble home in a couple of hours, and Zoey wondered if she should put in earplugs. She was approaching Vilma and Agnes's house when a bright green light filled the sky.

Zoey shielded her eyes with her hand and tried to locate the source of the light. The green light grew as if it were a large bubble in the night sky and Zoey gasped with worry when she saw it was coming from Vilma and Agnes's backyard. Worry turned to fear when Zoey heard a scream echo through the quiet of the night.

"Vilma! Agnes! I'm coming," Zoey yelled as she darted down the road.

Zoey jumped the curb and ran across the dewy grass as the green light grew in intensity. The light engulfed her as she ran down the side of the house. The something in the light made her skin tingle as though she'd stuck her finger into an electrical socket. Zoey struggled to breath and stumbled to a stop. What was this?

Zoey's hip hit the hose bracketed to the side of the house. Water! With her hands shaking and her eyes stinging, she turned on the hose. The water splashed onto her hands, bringing instant relief. Without hesitation, Zoey sprayed herself down with water. Water cleared the pain from her eyes and slowly Zoey could blink Vilma and Agnes into focus. Vilma's hands were outstretched, pain etched on her face, her entire elderly body shaking as the green light rose from the ground and shot out her hands. Agnes stood on Vilma's far side, holding out what looked like an urn.

Zoey followed the green light and saw it was directed at someone. A man, probably around Zoey's age, who towered over Vilma and Agnes as he tried to press against the green light with a light blue light of his own while he struggled to reach Vilma. He was dressed in black leather, but it was the tattoo on his neck that caught her attention. It was a tattoo of interlocking swords forming a circle with a drop of blood in the center, and it appeared to be glowing.

What Zoey saw didn't make sense. What was Vilma doing? How was she doing it? Why was there a monster of a man starting to glow brighter and brighter the closer and closer the green light got to him?

Vilma looked ready to pass out, and Zoey gave up trying to understand what was happening. She opened her mouth to scream, but the tattoo became so bright it began to smoke. Agnes stepped forward holding the urn, the man yelling in pain as a blue light shot from his throat, and Zoey screamed.

In that one moment, two things happened: Zoey accidently sprayed the hose and soaked Vilma and Agnes, and second, the light stopped heading toward Agnes's urn and slammed into Zoey's open mouth. A moment before Zoey's mind went blank, she saw the hulking man fall to the ground. Vilma and Agnes stepped forward, and with a flick of their fingers, the man burst into flames.

4
_____

"WELL, if that didn't just get mucked up," Zoey heard Agnes mutter.

"What do you think it means?" Vilma whispered.

"You don't suppose it's *in* her, do you?" Agnes asked.

"Where else would it be? We saw it enter her. Let's just hope she doesn't figure it out before we can decide what to do," Vilma said a moment before Zoey felt the splash of water on her face.

Zoey sputtered, her eyes popping open as water streamed onto her face.

"Oh, here she is." Vilma turned off the hose. "Can you hear me, dear?" she asked loudly.

Zoey's head felt as if it were floating like a balloon while her whole body tingled. She struggled to sit up as she nodded her head. "What's going on? What happened to the guy?"

"What guy, dear?" Vilma asked innocently.

"What do you mean, what guy?" Zoey raised her voice as Agnes helped her sit up. "The guy you were shooting with green light out of your fingers, who then burst into flames. That's who!"

Agnes and Vilma looked worriedly at each other as Zoey looked frantically around for the burning man.

"Oh, dear. We better call the doctor," Agnes said softly to Vilma. "I think she's hit her head."

"I didn't hit my head!" Zoey defended as her eyes frantically took in the completely normal backyard. There were no strange lights, there was no burning man, and no fire at all. Not even leftover smoke.

"Yes, Agnes, I think we better."

Zoey looked around. Her head was swimming. Could it all have been a dream? Had she tripped over the hose at her feet and hit her heard and made it all up? "No, don't call an ambulance. They're probably tied up at the park. When I left, a full-out riot had erupted between the Irises and the Opossums. Were you in the backyard? Did I trip over the hose?"

The women nodded.

"That's it!" Vilma said with a relieved smile.

"We were back here watering flowers and talking when you came around the side of the house and tripped on the hose. Poor dear. Let's get you inside and get some ice on your head."

The two old women reached down and, with surprising agility, helped Zoey up. They directed her into the house with each of them holding on to an arm. Something nagged at her as they led her through the backdoor.

"Wait, there are no flowers in your backyard," Zoey said as she stopped so suddenly the two women almost tripped.

"Oh!" Vilma looked panicked as Agnes pushed Zoey into the house. Zoey saw Agnes wiggle her fingers as she lurched past the doorway.

"She must have hit her head harder than we thought," Agnes worried. "She can't see all the flowers in the backyard. Dear, is your vision blurry? Do you see four of us?"

Zoey broke from Agnes's grip and looked out the sliding glass door and into a yard filled with flowers overflowing from large pots on the patio. "Maybe you better call the doctor. I would have sworn you didn't have any flowers." Zoey muttered.

Agnes and Vilma shared a look before helping Zoey to lie down on their floral print couch. Her head rested on big pink magnolia blooms as she closed her eyes and tried to figure out where exactly her head hurt. But she didn't hurt. In fact, she felt as if she were in a pleasant haze as her body hummed with a warm energy.

"I think I'll close my eyes for a little while. I'm suddenly really sleepy." Zoey closed her eyes and before she drifted off to sleep she felt a crocheted afghan being draped over her.

$$\sim$$

ZOEY STRETCHED and felt the blanket sliding down her body. When she opened her eyes, two pairs of eyes were staring at her from the small kitchen. Vilma and Agnes looked relieved. They set down their morning tea and hurried to the couch.

"How are you feeling, dear?" Agnes asked as she peered over Zoey as if searching for an answer in her face.

Zoey thought about it for a moment as she checked her body. She moved her arms, legs, and rolled her head from side to side. "I seem to be all better. What time is it?"

"Seven thirty," Vilma answered as a cup of tea was shoved into Zoey's hand.

Zoey almost spilled it as she shot upright. "I have to go! I have so much baking to do before I open!"

"*Tsk*, you should have some tea. It'll make you right as rain," Vilma said as she shoved the cup into Zoey's hand again.

Zoey had to get to her shop and didn't have time to argue. She had learned to pick her battles in life and this wasn't one of them. So she grabbed the tea and tossed it back as if it were a shot of tequila. She handed the empty cup to Vilma and hurried out the door.

ZOEY DIDN'T EVEN bother to go home. She jogged straight toward her shop. She hadn't gotten far when she noticed how quiet the town still was. She decided it was for one of two reasons: the townspeople were still hung over from last night or they were in jail.

Zoey looked into Peach's house as she jogged by to see if Otis had come home yet, and it caused her to trip. Zoey's arms flapped in the air, but it didn't help her fly. The concrete came at her fast as her hands and knees hit first. What the blazes did she trip over?

Zoey groaned as she sat back on her heels and brushed her skinned palms off on her thighs before looking behind her. Zoey opened her mouth on a silent gasp. There, lying across the sidewalk outside of Peach's house was Tim Hildebrand, the recipe master at Moonshine Distillery.

Tim lay with his head turned at a weird angle, his eyes open, locked in surprise and staring at her. Zoey's breath came in shallow little gasps as she inched closer to Tim's body on her hands and knees. Her body tingled with fear as she reached out with shaking fingers to check his pulse . . . but she never got the chance. Something that felt like fire shooting from her fingertips made her fingers burn and then *poof,* Tim was gone.

"What the . . .?" Zoey looked frantically around. Where did Tim go?

Zoey was on her hands and knees looking under Peach's azalea bush when she heard a man chuckle behind her.

"Tim?" Zoey asked, slightly panicked as she whipped around. "I'm going to kill you. What a horrible prank . . . Oh, Luke. Um, hi?" Zoey sat back on her heels and pulled an azalea branch from her hair.

Luke had a smile across his face as he looked down at her. "Care to tell me what you're doing digging around under Peach's bush and why you thought I was Tim?"

Zoey let out a huff of air to get the hair away from her eyes. "I think I'm seeing things. Maybe Vilma and Agnes were right, maybe I do need to see a doctor."

Luke raised an eyebrow. "Why would you need to see a doctor?"

"I fell last night and hit my head. I've been seeing things that aren't there ever since. Like a man going up in flames. Or a dead person lying across the sidewalk," Zoey told him.

The smile fell from Luke's face. "I think they're right. Let me take you to see the doctor."

Zoey wrinkled her nose. "But Dr. Thurman is like ninety years old and smells of mothballs and antiseptic. And he doesn't do anything except tell you to put an icepack on everything from cuts to heart attacks," Zoey complained.

"Too bad, I'm taking you," Luke said seriously as he reached down and helped her up.

Zoey let herself be helped up and escorted to the cruiser. It took all of two minutes to get to Dr. Thurman's office, located a block off Main Street. Doris Bleacher was the secretary. She sat in the same olive green vinyl chair she'd been sitting in since the 1970s and wore a disapproving look on her pinched face. Her gray hair was pulled into a bun on the top of her head.

The office and its occupants were stuck in the wrong decade. Neither Doris nor Dr. Thurman looked as if they realized time had passed since bellbottoms and burnt colors went out of fashion. Dr. Thurman wore either polyester or seersucker and usually in dark gold, maroon, or puke green. Doris wasn't any better with her large paisley dresses and cat's eye bejeweled glasses.

"Can I help you?" Doris asked in her nasally voice. She sounded annoyed anyone would actually dare come into the doctor's office.

"Yes, this is Zoey Mathers. She fell and hit her head last night and has been seeing things ever since. I was hoping Doc Thurman was in to take a look at her," Luke said as he helped Zoey into a burnt gold plastic love seat.

"I'll see if he has an opening," Doris said before getting up and walking through a door to the back office.

Luke took a seat next to Zoey and looked at her with concern in his eyes. "Is there anything I can help you with? Are you feeling okay?"

"I'm really feeling fine, I'm just seeing things is all," Zoey said with a shake of her head. Could today get any weirder?

The back door opened and Doris looked mad at having to show them back to the exam room. The olive green exam table was covered in stiff paper so old it was turning yellow. Zoey sat on the edge of the table and cringed as the paper crackled loud through the room. Luke took a cautious seat in the plastic chair with rusted legs.

The sound of a thumping cane had them turning toward

the door. The end of the cane came into view first, followed by Dr. Thurman's shuffling feet. Today he was in burnt orange, gold, and olive green plaid pants with a mustard yellow shirt and brown suspenders. He headed over to Luke and bent down to look into his eye.

"Eh, you don't look like you have a concussion. Here, put an ice pack on your head for twenty minutes and you'll be right as rain."

"Um, I'm not the one who is injured," Luke said as he pointed to Zoey.

"Eh? Oh, oh, okay," Dr. Thurmond turned to shuffle over to Zoey and looked into her eyes before yanking the ice pack from Luke's hand and shoving it into hers. "Twenty minutes and you'll be right as rain. You can pay Doris on the way out."

Zoey put the ice pack to her head and sighed. "Well, I might as well get my money's worth."

5
_____

ZOEY PUT the key into the back door of her shop and unlocked it. She hated to admit it, but the ice pack had made her feel better. Luke had dropped her at the bakery and headed to the sheriff's office. Zoey was way behind on work. It would be a very busy day since she was already late opening for the day. Luckily the town was also running late, having partied well into the night. Luke had told her the food fight finally ended when free drinks of the moonshine entries were handed out.

Zoey pushed the back door open, flipped on the light, and screamed. Tim Hildebrand was lying on her prep table. His glassy eyes stared at her and his neck was twisted in the same odd angle as it had been when she saw him on the sidewalk.

Zoey closed her eyes. "This isn't real. This isn't real," she chanted. When she slowly opened her eyes Tim was still there. Okay, maybe this was real. He sure did look real. Maybe she should run down to the sheriff's department?

Zoey took a tentative step forward to get a closer look at Tim's body. He had been choked and his neck was possibly broken. It appeared Tim had put up a struggle. Zoey took in the bruises around his neck, the way his nails on his hands were chipped and knuckles bruised, and the fact that his suit jacket pocket was torn open. A small torn off corner of a piece of paper was stuck in the stitching of the pocket.

Bending down, Zoey reached out to see what was on the paper. Her fingers warmed and the second Zoey touched Tim, *poof!* He was gone.

"Not again!" Zoey yelled as she slammed her hands onto the bare prep table. "No, I'm not crazy," she said to the baking equipment she had sitting out around the kitchen.

Pulling out her phone she searched for Tim's phone number and paced the kitchen as the phone rang and rang. Voicemail picked up and Zoey hung up. She was scared she was going crazy and there was one way to prove she wasn't. She was going to find Tim Hildebrand, but it would have to wait until after her marathon baking session.

THE FRONT DOOR opened an hour later and Zoey hurried out from the back to find Vilma and Agnes perusing the freshly stocked displays. "Hey ladies," Zoey wiped her hands on her apron and opened the display.

"There are too many choices, dear," Agnes said as she kept her nose plastered to the glass in order to get a close look at the desserts.

"How are you feeling?" Vilma asked.

"Hey, do you all know Tim Hildebrand?" Zoey asked instead of answering.

"Of course we do," Agnes said from her place of dessert inspection.

"He's the recipe holder at the distillery," Vilma added. "It's his job to hold on to the recipes for all the moonshine ever made. Last night, he was the one all the groups gave their moonshine flavor of the year recipes to for judging. Tim compares them to all the previous recipes and all the flavors other distilleries produce to make sure the special flavor isn't already taken. Then we vote. Why?"

"Has anyone seen him since last night?" Zoey asked them.

"I don't know. He lives alone over on Double Run," Agnes said into the glass. "I'll take the chocolate raspberry brownie."

"There is something very strange going on," Zoey said as she reached for the brownie but then froze in thought. "If I tell you, you'll think I'm crazy. Heck, *I* think I'm crazy."

Vilma and Agnes gasped.

"What?" Zoey asked as the women stared wide eyed. "Don't tell me Tim is standing behind me."

The women didn't need to answer for she saw it a second later. A pink plate with a brownie and fork on it was floating over the display case straight into Agnes's hands. "Nope, that's not real. I'm just seeing things," Zoey said out loud to herself as she closed her eyes and shook her head.

"Um," Vilma started to say but Zoey cut her off.

"Please don't tell me to go see Dr. Thurmond," Zoey groaned. "I think I need to see someone in Knoxville. I only hope they don't lock me away. First I see a dead body and when I reach for it, it disappears. That happened not once, but twice. I found the dead body in my kitchen. *Poof*, gone again the second I touch it. Don't know where Tim is now. And then I see a brownie floating. I need help."

"Oh, dear," Vilma muttered.

"We need to tell her," Agnes said softly.

"You don't need to tell me I'm crazy. I know it," Zoey cried as she flung her hands up into the air.

"Um, actually, you're not," Agnes hedged.

"You saw it?" Zoey asked quickly.

"I am eating the brownie, aren't I?" Agnes smiled.

"Maybe you should come over here and sit down," Vilma suggested.

Zoey couldn't believe it. They saw the brownie. The brownie had floated out of the display case, onto a plate, gotten a fork, and floated over to Agnes. Zoey had thought about getting the brownie and doing just that, but she had been in the middle of her worried rant and hadn't actually done it. Now that she thought about it, she had felt her fingers warming when she reached toward the display before stopping. And she'd felt her fingers turn hot when she had reached for Tim both times. Zoey raised her hands and stared at her fingers. They appeared to be okay. No burns, no flames, nothing. Just normal fingers. And why wasn't Agnes and Vilma freaking out like she was?

"Come on, dear," Agnes said softly. The duo had come behind the counter and were pulling Zoey into the back kitchen.

"Have a seat." Vilma pushed her onto the stool she kept for long hours decorating her concoctions. "There's something we need to tell you."

"Just rip it off, like a Band-Aid," Agnes instructed.

"It's not that easy," Vilma hissed back.

"Sure it is." Agnes stepped forward and stood in front of Zoey. "Dear, you're a witch now. See? Easy peasy."

Zoey blinked. She opened her mouth then closed it again. Was she hearing things? "I'm sorry, could you repeat that?"

Agnes looked annoyed. "Witch. You're a finger wiggling, all-powerful witch."

Nope, Zoey hadn't misheard her. Maybe she wasn't the crazy one. "So, you're like Wiccan and want to convert me?"

Vilma snorted. "We're not Wiccan. We're older than those youngsters. We are the Claritase."

Agnes patted Zoey's hands and drew her attention back to her. "See, back in the ancient world, witches were healers. The Goddess imparted the gift to a select few men and women to heal the pains of a growing new world. Over the millennium, some were killed off during various famines, wars, and disasters. And of course we lost quite a few during the witch hunts. We went into hiding after that terrible time. The man you saw us with last night is one of the Tenebris hunters. They are a group of men imbued with the power of the Goddess, just like us, but five hundred years ago they got a new leader, and since then they are no longer content sharing that power. See, if you kill a witch, you can consume the power of that witch."

Zoey blinked again. She felt her head shaking as Agnes rolled on with her story.

"Tenebris hunters roam the world trying to find the few remaining Claritase to take our powers so they can grow stronger. Vilma was using the power of Earth to defeat him. The hunter, with the pale blue light, had the power of Air."

Zoey increased the pace of her headshaking. "This is crazy! You aren't ancient witches. You're two little old ladies."

"Ladies, yes," Agnes agreed.

"Witches, definitely. Old, definitely. Thousands of years or so." Vilma wiggled her fingers and every appliance turned on. She wiggled them again and *poof,* cupcakes lined the prep table. "Do you need more examples? I can pop us over to Tuscany real fast. It's beautiful this time of year."

"You can't . . ." *Poof!* Zoey looked around. Vilma was gone. Just like that, she disappeared. *Poof.* Zoey was standing with Vilma in front of her again with a bottle of red wine being shoved into her hand.

Zoey stared down at the bottle as Agnes gave a little flick of her fingers and the cork popped out. So Zoey did the only thing she could think of. She put the bottle to her lips and drank until her body tingled with alcohol.

She set the bottle down on the counter and took a deep breath. Her mind was going in twenty different directions at once and none of them led to anything that made sense. "Okay, so you two are thousands of years old witches with powers derived from a goddess, and you're being hunted by bad guys who want to steal your powers. Where in all of this did I suddenly become a witch?"

"Well, it may sound a little strange . . ." Vilma started.

"Oh, yeah, it's only going to sound strange now," Zoey snorted.

Vilma ignored her. "As I said, there are few of us left—less than two hundred all over the world. The Tenebris somehow found Agnes and me and sent a hunter to take our powers. The only way to take our power is to use the strength from the elements and pull their powers from their bodies. It was the light you saw coming from the hunter. It will go where directed, which was supposed to be the urn, but when you doused us with water my powers temporarily sputtered since I was drawing on Earth power, not Water power. Therefore, the man's powers went to the nearest open object—your open, screaming mouth," Vilma said not too pleased.

"So, water stops your power?"

"Not really. When we draw our powers, we draw from one of the elements—Earth, Water, Fire, or Air. Opposing elements can temporarily interfere until we redirect our powers to handle that new element. It's physically and mentally exhausting having one of these struggles for power," Vilma explained.

"And now I have this guy's power?" Zoey asked, struggling to believe any of this.

The two women nodded. "But it doesn't make sense that you can actually use it," Vilma told her.

Agnes shook her head. "We'll have to look into that. But you'll need to learn to control these powers," Agnes warned.

"I don't want to control it. Take it back. You said you wanted to take that guy's powers, so take them from me." Zoey jumped off the stool. This was the perfect answer, because right now she was beyond freaked out. An ancient battle of good versus evil, people living over a thousand years, wiggling fingers to move objects . . . no. She didn't want this.

"I'm sorry, dear," Vilma told her and she leaned forward and patted her hand. "But to take someone's powers means killing them. That's what happened to the man you saw before we burnt him and gave his ashes back to the Goddess."

"See?" Agnes asked softly. "If we take the powers from you, you will die."

And then, for the second time in twenty-four hours, Zoey fainted.

6

WATER SPLASHED over Zoey's face again. When she sputtered and opened her eyes she almost wished she hadn't. One of her mixing bowls was floating in the air with drops of water plunking on the floor from where it had just magically dumped water on her.

"I'm a witch," Zoey stated seriously.

The two old lady heads bobbed.

"And I don't mean to diminish the importance of this discovery, especially since you'll now become hunted as a member of Claritase, but did you mention a dead body?" Agnes reminded her.

Zoey took a deep breath. She was going to do what she did best as a lawyer—she was going to compartmentalize. Zoey would pretend all this witch stuff didn't exist, and she'd deal with it later. "Yes. I tripped over Tim Hildebrand this morning outside Peach's house. He was dead. It looked as if he'd been choked and I think his neck was broken. I went to feel for a pulse but my fingers warmed and *poof*, Tim disappeared only to reappear in my kitchen."

Zoey saw Vilma and Agnes share a look of surprise. Although, Zoey didn't think the look of surprise was over Tim's dead body. "What?" Zoey asked finally.

"Um, it's just that being new to your powers you shouldn't be able to move something as big as a body. Snap and light a candle, sure. Move a pencil, sure. But a two hundred pound man? That usually takes newbies decades to master," Vilma said with confusion.

Agnes nibbled on her lip. "She didn't just move him, Vilma, she transported him to where she was thinking."

"What does that mean?" Zoey asked, not knowing if she really wanted an answer.

"It means you're way more powerful than the average witch, especially when you shouldn't have the powers to begin with. We'll need to look into this. But first, tell us more about Tim," Vilma said.

"I noticed a ripped edge of a piece of paper in his torn coat pocket and I noticed he had defensive wounds. His nails were broken and bloody. He had fought back," Zoey told them.

"When you were reaching for him," Agnes hedged, "what exactly were you thinking?"

Zoey thought back as if Tim was in front of her. She reached her fingers forward remembering. "I was thinking I wanted to see what the paper was before I called the sheriff."

Vilma and Agnes groaned.

"What?"

"The way transport works is if you send energy while thinking of a location, that's where the object will go," Agnes told her.

Zoey gasped. "You're telling me I *poofed* Tim to the sheriff's office?"

She didn't wait for a response before throwing open the back door and dashed her way down Main Street. She noticed but didn't want to think about the fact that Vilma and Agnes were easily keeping up with her. Could her life get anymore messed up?

Yes. Yes it could.

LUKE STOOD with his hands on his hips outside the station looking at Tim Hildebrand's dead body where it sat leaning against the station door. Zoey would have kept going, but a wrinkled old hand with the power of some goddess yanked her back into the entrance of the hardware store. The three of them peered around the wall where they were shielded from view and watched as the sheriff pulled to a stop and joined Luke, who was standing hands on hips, staring at Tim.

"Oh my god," Zoey groaned.

"Goddess," Vilma and Agnes absently corrected.

"Whatever! Tim's propped up against the door like he was placed there!"

"He was. You put him there," Vilma responded matter-of-factly.

"We need a reason to get closer," Agnes told them.

"I normally bring muffins, but I haven't had time to make them yet," Zoey said as she watched the sheriff make a phone call.

"Well, whip them up," Vilma ordered.

"You mean I can do that?" Zoey asked in wonder.

"If you can transport Tim, you can certainly make some muffins," Agnes confirmed.

"Then why do you come to my store every day when you

can just whip up your favorite desserts with a flick of your fingers?"

Vilma shook her head. "Doesn't work like that. Magic comes from within. If I made muffins they would taste as if I made them at home and trust me when I say I can't make them nearly as well as you do. But you have the recipes inside you. The magic will use it. So, focus on what you want to appear and let your body work."

Zoey closed her eyes and focused on muffins. In her mind she saw the ingredients, saw how she mixed them, saw the finished product. Her fingers warmed and she gave them a wiggle. When she opened her eyes Vilma was holding a platter of muffins.

"No way!" Zoey sniffed them. They smelled just like her muffins.

"Now let's see what's going on." Agnes shoved Zoey forward.

She stumbled onto the sidewalk, drawing Luke's and Sheriff Weller's attention. "Good morning," Zoey smiled. It was a fake smile, a smile that hid the fear that at any moment they would decry her a witch and burn her at the stake. "I brought muffins."

Luke stepped to block her path. "You shouldn't see this."

"Oh, what is it deputy?" Agnes asked all innocently.

"There's been a murder," Luke said, all business.

"Here? In Moonshine? Who is it?" Vilma asked as her hand fluttered to her heart.

"Tim Hildebrand."

The three of them gasped. Okay, maybe being a lawyer was good practice for being a witch.

"Do you know who did it?" Zoey asked.

"Not yet. But, there have been reports of hearing a loud

motorcycle driving through town early this morning. Not too many motorcycles registered here. Don't know if it means anything, but I'll look into. In the meantime I've called in the state police to help me process the area. I'm sorry, I need to ask you to stay clear of the area so we don't contaminate anything."

"Make sure to put the muffins in the cruiser!" Sheriff Weller yelled, his white mustache waggling. He shot them a wave before resuming staring at Tim with his hands on his hips.

Zoey handed the muffins to Agnes and Vilma who meandered over to the cruiser before making their way to Sheriff Weller to see if they could find out more. After all, they were of a similar age, or Zoey had thought so until she discovered the women were literally ancient.

"How are you feeling?" Luke asked gently as he walked over to her and looked her up and down as if he could see where she was hurting.

Zoey smiled in response. "Feel great. That ice pack set me to rights."

Luke's lips quirked, but he didn't contradict her. "I was going to see if you wanted to go to dinner tonight, but I have a feeling it's going to be a long day for me. Maybe I can get a rain check?"

"Sure, I'd like that," Zoey said and meant it. She'd never been out with a guy from outside of LA. It would be completely different, but that didn't mean it wouldn't be good. As long as she didn't *poof* him someplace by accident that is.

"Great. Hey, didn't you think you saw Tim this morning?"

"I had a head injury," Zoey reminded him with a shrug.

"True," he said, seemingly shrugging it off. "I'll call you when I get a chance to talk about dinner." Luke gave her a look that sent her fingers tingling and her eyes widening.

"I better get going," she thought before she zapped him straight to her bed.

7

ZOEY WAS BURIED up to her eyes in research. She'd read about Wiccans, read about the Salem witch trials, and watched the whole first season of *Bewitched*. She thought she was getting the hang of this being-a-witch thing. She thought so until Agnes and Vilma brought over a "couple" of books for her to read. Those couple of books turned into a complete set of Claritase encyclopedias starting from the first witch and going all the way until last year.

While the read was a lot more interesting than case law, some of the centuries *could* have been summarized. Zoey's eyes felt gritty. She'd stayed up all night reading, but now she felt she had an understanding of the history and role the Claritase played. However, the Claritase had lain low during the last four hundred years. That was when the Tenebris had started hunting them and used the Salem witch trials as a way to flush them out. The Tenebris had worked side by side with the Claritase, but then they elected a new leader, Alexander, in 1518. Alexander believed the Claritase were inferior to the Tenebris. To Zoey it sounded as if he didn't like being less powerful than some of the Claritase and wanted their power

Four hundred years ago, a contingent of witches lead by Grand Mistress Helena had met with Alexander under a white flag to negotiate a truce only to be killed by Alexander and his council. When the others Tenebris members saw the power that could be obtained by killing another witch, they leapt into the hunt Alexander continued to wage.

Since then, the witches had never gathered as one again. Instead they sent in reports and the master secretary recorded it into the official history book. All history books held by the Claritase members would magically update after each official entry. They had a better updating system than any smartphone.

But what really worried Zoey was the Tenebris. Vilma and Agnes told her they wouldn't think to look for a third witch in Moonshine Hollow, but if discovered, Zoey would have to learn to protect herself. Witch lessons started that night.

In the meantime, she had more sweet treats to bake than she could shake a broom at; which, she was saddened to learn last night, witches didn't actually fly on.

~

ZOEY DECIDED to take the long way to her shop. The sun wasn't quite up, but the darkness was beginning to turn to the early glow of dawn as she turned onto Double Run. Tim's house was the second house on the left. It was easy to spot with the yellow crime scene tape over the door. She didn't really know what she was looking for. She just felt the need to look around.

She slowed her pace and looked around. Not many

lights were on yet, and those that were on were in the back of houses as people were getting up. She didn't know why, but she felt responsible for Tim. Maybe it was because she'd zapped him all over town.

Zoey stood in front of the house, not knowing what to do first. What she really wanted was to figure out what the piece of paper in his pocket was. Was it part of a recipe? An overdue water bill? Zoey turned around and looked at the mailbox. Why not start the day off with a felony?

She opened the mailbox and held her breath. Her heart was pounding as if the killer would leap out right then and there. When she looked inside she was unreasonably disappointed to find it empty. But then she heard it. The slight sound of leaves rustling. There was someone nearby.

Zoey looked around quickly. By the porch of the one story brick house was the beginning of a row of azalea bushes lining the side of the house heading toward the backyard. Tiptoeing forward, she zeroed in on the bush right under a small square window.

The leaves moved and Zoey worked hard to stifle the scream. With a shaking hand, she reached to move the branches. Her hand hadn't touched the green leaves or red blooms when they burst open. Several thoughts went through her head at once. Was it the murderer? Was she going to die with her throat slit in the middle of the street after dragging her dying body out there to get help? Why had she come here? And was she wearing clean underwear?

Her fingers tingled and *poof!* The object flying toward her throat vanished. Zoey blinked and put both hands over her throat to feel for blood. Nothing. She'd sent the threat magically through space to . . . the middle of the road.

Zoey leapt up, grabbed a garden gnome statue holding a bottle of moonshine, and ran for the road. Instead of the knife-wielding man she expected to see, she found a black Labrador puppy sitting in the middle of the road looking as confused as Zoey felt. Her face flushed red with embarrassment. She guessed the row of sharp puppy teeth was the knife she thought she saw and the blood was really the cute pink tongue the little black puppy was using to lick the hurt paw it was holding up gingerly.

"Oh, you poor thing," Zoey cooed as she dropped to her knees and slowly began to crawl toward the little puppy still sitting in the road.

The puppy looked startled, but didn't move as Zoey continued to talk softly and crawl closer. The pup stopped licking its paw and stared at her. It looked ready to bolt at any second but held still, watching Zoey instead.

"It's okay. I won't hurt you. I promise," Zoey said soothingly as she crawled across the pavement, hoping the hurt puppy wouldn't run and hoping she wouldn't zap the poor thing again.

"Here you go, sweet thing. I'll make it all better," Zoey comforted as the pup let her reach out and pet him.

"Too bad you're not talking to me," the deep voice said from behind her, startling the puppy. The puppy jumped again and Zoey knew it wasn't a knife-wielding murderer so she managed not to *poof* the little dog away again. Instead of jumping away from Zoey, the puppy jumped into her arms at the sound of Luke's voice.

"You scared him." Zoey lifted the shaking puppy up into her arms. "What are you doing sneaking around?"

Luke grinned at the scowl Zoey sent him over her shoulder. "I'm pretty sure I wasn't the only one sneaking around. I got a call about a potential burglar peeking into Tim's house right after I got a call about seeing a stranger on a motorcycle."

"Oh," Zoey said with an innocent blink of her eyes. "Well, surely you don't mean me? I've been trying to rescue this poor hurt puppy, and I certainly don't have a motorcycle."

Luke looked as if he didn't believe her. "I'll call the pound to come take it away."

"No, he has a hurt paw. Don't call the pound. I'll have the vet fix him up and take care of him. I'd hate to think of him locked up in a cage with no one to love him."

Zoey kissed the top of the puppy's head. "I would think you would be too busy to take a nosy neighbor call. Have you learned anything about what happened to Tim?"

Luke's smile slid into a look that was coldly serious. "It was murder. He was strangled from behind, as if he were in a chokehold. His neck was broken, probably after he passed out from suffocation, and we found a piece of paper in his pocket that was the edge of a recipe."

"Do you think he was murdered for the moonshine recipes?" Zoey asked as she held the puppy closer to her chest as if to protect the innocent life.

"It appears that way. I'm meeting with Ronald Stone, the owner of Stonecreek Distillery, this morning."

Zoey nodded. Stonecreek was the main rival of Moonshine Distillery. They were on the other side of the mountain in the small town of Stonecreek. From the same headwaters high up on the mountain, creeks flowed down opposite sides of the mountain and through both towns to feed the distilleries. Folklore told that Ned Earnest, the founder of Moonshine Hollow, and Elijah Stone were cousins who traveled into the frontier together. All was well until one night their grandfather took ill and called both boys into the family's small cabin. Ned was the first to arrive, and fearing he wouldn't make it, the grandfather told Ned the family recipe for his moonshine. Ned left when Elijah arrived, and shortly after their grandfather passed away.

The rift began when Ned and Elijah began making their moonshine. Somehow they were not the same. Each claimed to be the original recipe handed down from their grandfather, but the two were completely opposite in taste. Over time, Ned's moonshine became more popular and Elijah's and Ned's families became competitors. Rumor had it in the last couple of years, Ronald Stone had tanked the family distillery when he tried to corner the health market with kale and quinoa moonshines.

"You think Ronald had Tim killed to get the recipes?" Zoey asked as Luke held out his hand and helped her up from the street.

"I think someone had Tim killed for all the recipes. I still can't find this mysterious guy on a motorcycle that one of Tim's neighbors called about twenty minutes ago. When we searched Tim's office, we discovered the entire history of recipes from Moonshine Distillery were gone. When I talked to Mr. Earnest, he said Tim always carried them on him to keep them safe. He confirmed that the paper in Tim's pocket was part of a recipe from the master collection." Luke let go of her hand and put his hands on his hips as he looked down at the puppy now asleep in her arms. "I think this dog was meant to be yours. It was fate you found him."

A sudden vision of another man, this one taller, darker, broader, and more muscular than Luke shot through her mind, saying something similar about fate. Zoey felt chills run down her spine at the same time her body flushed hot. Zoey shook her head to dislodge the image of Slade in black pleather and a tight T-shirt.

"I think I'll name him Chance," Zoey said, stroking the pup's head. She saw Luke's eye soften as he watched her, and Zoey suddenly felt guilty for the images of Slade that had caused her whole body to shiver. But what caused that shiver? "Luke, would you let me know how it goes with Ronald? I can't help but feel somewhat responsible for Tim." Especially since she's zapped her all over town.

"I didn't realize you two were close," Luke said, his eyes sharpening.

"We weren't," Zoey said slowly as she tried to pull anything out of the air to explain herself. "He, uh, he came into my bakery quite often and was such a nice man."

Luke nodded his agreement. "Yes, he was. I better get going to meet Mr. Stone. I was hoping I would see you at Mountaineers later tonight."

"I'm meeting Maribelle there, so I will see you then."

"I'll let you know tonight what I find out over in Stonecreek."

Chance licked her face as Zoey watched Luke drive off. "Well, Chance, I'm in trouble. I have a half a day to get a full day's worth of work in. I'll never fulfill my orders in time. But at least I'll have you for company."

Chance wagged his long tail as Zoey headed to her bakery. Murder didn't stop gossip. It only fueled it. Zoey would need to prepare a lot of food to feed the people of this town, all with murder on their minds.

8

"I CAN DO THIS," Zoey chanted as she peeked around the wall and out the front window. A line of people were standing on the sidewalk talking frantically, with their hands moving, as the gossip of Tim's death and the missing recipes tore through the town.

Zoey ducked her head back into the kitchen and stared at the empty trays that were supposed to be filled with croissants, scones, and muffins. "I can do this," Zoey repeated as she closed her eyes. She envisioned flour, sugar, eggs, chocolate chips, and more. Her fingers warmed, and she squeezed her eyes tighter as she felt the energy flying from her fingers. When the sizzle ended and her fingers went from hot back to normal, Zoey opened her eyes. Perfect chocolate chip muffins sat on the trays.

"Holy sugar drops," Zoey whispered as she heard a knock on the front door. It was time to open and Zoey only had one option. She closed her eyes and zapped up some white chocolate raspberry muffins and the rest of the breakfast menu and hoped to goodness the magical pastries didn't kill anyone.

Zoey grabbed a tray of scones and slid it into the display case on her way to open the door. Agnes and Vilma were first in line as half the town somehow managed to cram into her small bakery. "I need help," Zoey called over the crowd. Agnes and Vilma somehow heard her and headed for the kitchen to carry the trays out to the displays.

"Did you hear the news?" Maribelle asked as she stood on tiptoes and leaned over the display case.

Zoey nodded. "Poor Tim," Zoey said, reaching into the case to retrieve a muffin.

"No, not that," Maribelle whispered. "That's what everyone else is talking about. What I'm talking about is the hunka-hunka diamond on Missy's finger."

"Wayne and Missy are engaged?" Zoey gasped. Who would ever agree to marry that sleazeball?

"Right? They've dated eight days, but I think they're keeping it quiet since Missy's Pawpaw doesn't approve of Wayne. I saw the ring as she left her home. As soon as she saw me, she slipped it off and put it in her purse."

Zoey shuttered. "I can't imagine being married to Wayne. He's constantly scheming. I would always be worried he'd ditch me the second a better model came around or invest in every get rich quick plan."

"I think Missy's that get rich plan. Her daddy's loaded. Coal money, you know," Maribelle said conspiratorially as she paid Zoey.

Zoey nodded and sent her friend a smile as Maribelle took her muffin to join a group of Mountaineers waiting in the back of the line.

"Did you hear the news?" Peach asked in a hushed tone as she approached the display case as if not everyone else waiting in line was gossiping about the exact same thing.

"About Tim?" Zoey asked, slightly unsure after her conversation about Wayne and Missy.

Peach nodded. "It got me so scared I made Otis come home this morning. Can you imagine a killer running around Moonshine Hollow?" Peach pointed to a chocolate croissant and a bran muffin. "But I'm not going to feel bad for eating this yummy croissant in front of him. He needs to watch his sugar intake after all." Peach smirked.

Zoey pulled out the order as Peach leaned even closer and dropped her voice. "You know who I think it is? I think it was Doris Bleacher."

Zoey's eyebrows rose as she handed over her bag. "Dr. Thurman's Doris?" No way. Zoey couldn't imagine Doris doing anything besides glaring at someone.

"There's rumor that she and Tim were having a May-December romance. You didn't hear it from me, but Doris is quite the cougar," Peach whispered as Zoey tried not to throw up in her mouth.

"*Doris*?" Zoey couldn't have heard that right.

"You betcha. She read a kinky book where a three-hundred-year-old vampire met this young thirty-year-old mortal man and ties him to her bed to have her wicked way with him. Doris started going to these *specialty* clubs in Knoxville. Sally June said she saw a women she swore to be Doris dressed in black sneaking from Tim's house early in the morning at the beginning of the summer."

Zoey blinked speechless. Tim wasn't a young buck, but he was decades younger than Doris and the image of Doris tying Tim up . . . Well, maybe she got rambunctious trying to bite his neck and accidently broke it.

"Oh, here she is. Act normal," Peach hissed as she grabbed her bag and tried not to stare while walking past Doris who had inched her way through the door.

Zoey blushed and turned back to the next person in line. "Mornin' Miss Zoey."

"Good morning, Billy Ray. What can I do you for?" Zoey asked, using one of her favorite southern phrases she had picked up since moving to Moonshine.

"I'll take one of them double chocolate muffins. Have you heard the news?" Billy Ray asked as he ran a hand over his long bushy beard.

"Yes, I daresay the whole town has now heard about Tim," Zoey said, reaching for the muffin.

"Hmm, it had to be Ronald Stone. He's slicker than a greased pig, and everyone knows he has run Stonecreek Distillery into the ground. But I was talking about Wayne and Missy. I heard she was in the family way. Her Pa was in the club last night and was drunker than a skunk saying the only way he'd allow his baby to marry that good-for-nothing Wayne was if she were pregnant. Then news was this morning she's engaged, so I guess there's a bun in that oven."

As a lawyer, Zoey excelled at rationale and logic, but there was little of that in Moonshine. "I hate to state the obvious, but they only started dating eight days ago. I'm pretty sure she can't tell if she's pregnant yet. Besides, Missy is too concerned with how she'd look in a wedding dress to get pregnant. However, I have to admit Ronald Stone does sound suspect. Anyone who tries to make a kale and quinoa moonshine just ain't right."

"Amen, sister," Billy Ray agreed as he headed over to the group of Opossums huddled with some Irises. Gossip brought the romance back to Moonshine that was for sure. Peach and Otis were back together, and Billy Ray slipped his hand around his wife's waist as he handed her the top of the muffin, which everyone knows is the best part.

"I think it was the sexy biker," Faye said next as she moved up to collect her muffins. "I saw him, you know?" Faye practically preened.

"I know Luke is looking for him. What does he look like?" Zoey asked as Faye's cheeks turned pink.

"His face was covered with a helmet, but the good Lord certainly blessed his body. He was wearing these tight black jeans and shirt. I could see *everything*. Well, thanks for the muffins." Faye handed her money over and raced to catch up with Peach.

"Hey, baby," Justin smirked. "I'll take a dozen."

That got Zoey's attention. Justin never came into the shop for one reason—he spent all his money on moonshine. Which lead to the reason he held odd jobs. He drank too much to hold a steady one. "That'll be twenty dollars," Zoey said, not reaching for the muffin until she actually saw the cash. But sure enough, Justin slapped a twenty on the counter.

"So, baby, I was thinking we could get some chow at the diner tonight. My treat." Justin winked, and Zoey hurried to duck down to grab the muffins. "You know, like a date."

Zoey cringed. It wasn't that Justin was bad, he just wasn't good. He sped through town, he whistled at women, and he spent all his money on guns and moonshine. "Sorry, I can't. I have plans with Agnes and Vilma." Zoey shoved the box of muffins at him and then called, "Next!"

Zoey looked away from Justin's surprised face and right into the hard-lined face of Doris. "I want to take a bite out of the white chocolate raspberry. Give me two."

Zoey had to duck her head as she reached into the case so Doris wouldn't see her red cheeks. Peach had put the image of Doris as a kinky vamp into her head and now Zoey couldn't get it out of her head.

"Here you go," Zoey said with a blank face in place. Doris slapped her money on the counter and headed out of the store. No chitchat for her.

THE REST of the day flew by. Accusations were flying on who could have murdered Tim and whether or not Missy was knocked up. Finally, at two in the afternoon, there was peace. Zoey's mind was racing with all she had heard. She may have done her best to leave the law behind her, but as she cleaned her kitchen and prepped for the desserts, she was preoccupied with running all the possible criminal scenarios through her mind. Unfortunately, there were too many scenarios, too many rumors, and too many suspects. However, there was one thing that stuck out—Ronald Stone.

The bell over the door tinkled and Zoey wiped her hands on her apron. When she came out from the kitchen, she saw Luke peering into the display case. "Deputy, what can I do you for?"

"The bourbon chocolate cupcake looks great. I'll take one of those, please. It's been a long day." Luke straightened up, and Zoey saw the tight lines around his mouth.

"Did you meet with Ronald Stone? It seems most people believe he's behind Tim's murder," Zoey said, reaching for the cupcake.

"I did."

"What about the mysterious motorcycle man?"

"He's a ghost." Luke sighed. "Can I ask you a question as a lawyer?" he asked.

"Of course."

"I'm wondering about how much evidence is needed to secure a conviction. Our town is so small; the biggest case our ancient prosecutor has seen in the last six months is a case of cow tipping. You're a big city lawyer, and I'd like to see what you think," Luke told her as he ran a hand over his face.

"I didn't practice criminal work, but one of my friends did, so I heard a lot about it. I'll see what I can do." Zoey handed Luke the cupcake then moved around to the front so she could take a seat at one of the small bistro tables across from Luke.

Luke settled his long frame into the seat and sighed. "The sheriff wants me to arrest Stone, but I don't think I have enough evidence. Stone refused to let me search his office to look for the recipes, but did tell me he's seen one of them."

"Seen one?" Zoey asked as questions formed. "When? In what format? Who showed him? Where were they?"

Luke chuckled as he took a bite of the cupcake. "He said a photo of one recipe was emailed to him last night from an anonymous email address. Stone did show me the email, but not the recipe. The email offered to sell the entire recipe collection for a million dollars. The seller said they'd be in touch soon to receive the answer and the money. The sheriff thought it was a red herring to throw us off since Stone refused to destroy the recipe."

"I'd tell Stone he needs to hand over the recipe, then confiscate his email account or else charge him with receiving stolen property and also being in violation of Moonshine Distillery's intellectual property rights. You can get a warrant for the email address of the sender, but it may take a while to track that person down." Zoey thought she'd feel alive talking about the law, but she didn't. Instead, it seemed more like a distant memory. Zoey took a deep breath. She didn't miss being a lawyer. That revelation slammed into her. If she wasn't going to be a lawyer again, what would she do? Would she stay in Moonshine baking her sweet treats? And then another reckoning hit her, just like a truck running her over and then backing up to make sure she was dead. She was a witch. She'd been called that a time or two, but now she was a finger-wiggling, bona fide magical witch.

Luke interrupted her epiphany as he laid a five on the table. "Thanks for the advice. I'll see if the state police have any tech experts who can help trace the email address. If all else fails, I can call in a favor from some of my old partners in Knoxville or see if my contacts in Keeneston, Kentucky have any ideas. Ava would know who to talk to. They're good at navigating the gray area of the law. I like the idea of treating the recipes as stolen property. I'd been thinking of this solely as a murder. At least I can try to protect Moonshine Distillery's legacy."

Luke stood but paused as he looked down at her. Zoey's heart sped up and her fingers tingled to reach out to him so she shoved them into her lap. That was until she heard Ava's name again. Who was she to him? "Have you ever thought of running for town prosecutor?"

Zoey thought about it and thought about her epiphany she'd just had. "At one point I would have leapt at it. But the excitement isn't there anymore. I'm happy to help when I can, but baking makes me happy."

Luke gave her soft smile. "I understand. I am a little disappointed I will continue to be hampered by Mr. Jenkins's daily naps, so I may be calling on you if I need any more legal advice. Plus, I still owe you a real date."

When Luke smiled, Zoey felt the warmth shoot from her fingers throughout her entire body. Oh my. She needed more witch lessons or she may accidently zap Luke if he kept smiling at her like that. She also needed answers about Ava.

"I look forward to it."

9

THE PULL WAS STRONG. His body pulsed. The power of witchcraft spun in the air around him. He looked down the mountain at the small town. Somewhere down there was what his body needed. No, his body demanded it. He would find her, for if he didn't . . .

~

ZOEY CLEANED up the kitchen and scooped Chance out of the fuzzy sheepskin blanket in his basket before starting for Vilma and Agnes's home. She might be an accidental witch, but she was growing more comfortable with her powers as the day went on. It was hard to explain and even harder to understand, but something about the powers flowing through her felt right. Now she just needed to learn how they worked.

Chance wiggled in her arms and Zoey put the pup down on the ground. He ran around yipping and playing between her legs. As Zoey approached Vilma and Agnes's house, Chance stopped wiggling. His hair stood in a sharp strip down his back and even down the length of his stiff tail. A low growl emanated from his throat as sharp little puppy teeth were exposed while he snarled into the wind.

Zoey stopped and picked up her puppy. She brought him close to her chest and held him protectively as she picked up her pace. By the time she was at their door, Zoey was practically running as she flung the door open not even bothering to knock. Vilma and Agnes didn't seem surprised as Zoey panted, all out of breath, and hurriedly locked the door.

"You feel it?" Agnes asked.

Zoey clung to Chance as she tried to get her breathing back under control. Her body shook with the power coursing through her. And was it getting bright in there?

"*Duck,* she's going to blow!" Vilma yelled as she and Agnes dove for the floor a second before a bright light shot through the house.

"OH DEAR, SHE'S OUT AGAIN."

Two fuzzy white heads slowly came back into view as something wet covered Zoey's face. Chance was standing on her chest, licking her face, as Vilma and Agnes peered down at her.

"What happened?" Zoey asked as she placed Chance onto the ground. "And why is there a white patch of hair on the end of his tail?"

"You had a power surge, hon," Vilma said, helping her up.

"Shot out of you and right through poor Chance until it left through his tail. Put a humdinger of a spot on my rug too." Agnes pointed to the hole in her rug that went well beyond the rug. It was a hole straight into the depths of the earth.

"I . . . I did that?" Zoey stammered as she carefully peered down the hole. Somewhere in the depths of the darkness she could hear running water.

"You're much stronger than we ever imagined. But first lesson, if you make a mess, you clean it up," Agnes said, picking up Chance and pointing to the crater in the floor.

"How can I possibly—?"

"If you did it, you can undo it," Vilma lectured. "It's just like baking. Close your eyes, imagine what it looked like before, and funnel your power."

Zoey took a deep breath and did exactly what Vilma had told her. When she opened her eyes the floor was fixed as if nothing had ever happened. "Now that there's no longer a hole in the living room, can someone tell me what that feeling was that came over me before I ran inside?"

Vilma and Agnes shared a silent look. "Someone is coming near and that was a built-in safety mechanism you felt, warning you that danger is near."

"Who is near?" Zoey asked as she felt a shiver run through her body again.

"The Tenebris. Someone has come to finish the job," Agnes said ominously.

Zoey blinked as everything she had read about the Tenebris ran through her head. Then she groaned. "They won't have to search for me. I'll just light the way straight to me."

"Not if we teach you how to control it. Agnes, put on a pot of tea. It's going to be a long night." Vilma rubbed her hands together, and Zoey was suddenly not so sure of herself after all.

~

ZOEY WAS TORN between two worlds. The world she'd grown up in and known her entire life and the world Vilma and Agnes had introduced her to over the past few days. As much as Zoey wanted to pretend it was all a dream, her internal witch alarm was denying her the luxury of sticking her head in the ground until she was ready to face the situation.

Zoey flipped the lock to her café as she downed another shot of espresso. Maribelle was jumping from foot to foot and knocking impatiently. Maribelle was normally composed in a low maintenance country girl way but she was completely flustered that morning. Her hair was sticking out in every direction and there were dark circles under her eyes.

"Maribelle, what is it? Are you okay?" Zoey asked as Maribelle pushed through the door and shoved ten dollars into Zoey's apron pocket.

"There, I've paid you a retainer. You're my attorney now, right?" Maribelle shot an anxious look out the front of the shop as she bounced from foot to foot.

"Mari, I'm not licensed in Tennessee. Slow down and just tell me what's going on." Zoey grabbed her friend's arms to draw her attention away from the windows and back to her.

"Sheriff Weller thinks I murdered Tim. He and Luke are out looking for me right now," Maribelle said so quickly Zoey was sure she misunderstood.

"Wait, they think you killed Tim? Why would they think that?" Zoey asked as calmly as possible. Maribelle had the crazed look in her eyes that her celebrity client, Scott Westerfield, used to have.

"They already arrested Dale. His mama called me to blame me for getting him wrapped up in this. It's all because I used to date Ronald Stone, but that ended right before you arrived in town. They think Dale and I worked together— Dale to get the recipes from Tim and me to sell them to Ronald since I know how bad off his company is."

Zoey crossed her arms over her chest as Maribelle paced the length of the display case. "What evidenced do they have to prove this theory?"

"I don't know! All I know is they think I masterminded this." Maribelle gasped, her whole body shaking with fear. Zoey turned to see Luke watching them as he walked past the window toward the door. "Help me, please Zoey," Maribelle cried as tears began to stream from her eyes.

The door opened as Zoey grasped her best friend's hand. Luke walked through the door and stopped with his hand resting on the butt of his gun as his face set in frown. "Maribelle, you need to come with me."

Zoey felt her friend tighten her grip on Zoey's hand to a near painful squeeze. Maribelle's whole body shook, and Zoey felt the power inside her surge. The need to protect her friend had her body humming, but lighting up downtown wouldn't be the way to do so. Zoey took a deep breath and envisioned an old-fashioned mercury thermometer. Vilma had taught her this trick somewhere around two in the morning. The temperature was how close she was to losing it like she did yesterday. In her mind she saw the levels of the thermometer dropping, and as a result Zoey felt her powers change from volcanic to a gentle flow coursing through her.

"Luke, do you really think this is necessary? What evidence do you have to arrest her?" Zoey demanded, stepping in front of her friend as if she could physically protect her.

"We found a copy of one of the recipes at Dale's house with Maribelle's name on it," Luke said seriously. "It matched the recipe that was emailed to Ronald Stone. Ron finally handed over the email when we threatened to arrest him."

"Which recipe?" Zoey asked.

"Cherry blossom," Luke told her, reaching for handcuffs.

"That's the stupidest thing I have ever heard," Zoey said, focusing hard to keep her powers in control. "Maribelle and Dale were in charge of the Mountaineers' recipe for the moonshine competition. Of course they had copies of it! But so did half the club."

"It's a direct tie, Zoey. I'm sorry, but Maribelle, I need you to come with me while we execute a search warrant on your house and all your electronical devices." Luke handed the warrant to Zoey who immediately flipped it open and read it.

"I'm sorry, Maribelle, but the judge signed off on it. Go with Luke, but don't say a single word except to request a lawyer, which I advise you to say right now."

Maribelle was shaking as she stepped forward. "I request my right to an attorney. Zoey, can you come with me?"

Luke looked grim. "I'm sorry, but Zoey isn't a lawyer here in Tennessee. I believe she should be, but until the time she has court or bar approval for practicing within our state, she can't act on your behalf. You'll have to call Harlan."

Maribelle looked with desperation to Zoey. "Not Harlan! I'd be better off representing myself."

"I'll figure something out. I promise," Zoey vowed as

Luke escorted Maribelle out of the bakery as he read through her rights.

Zoey watched as her friend disappeared from view. What could she do to help? She needed to call Harlan, who was not her favorite person. When people got tired of the law she thought they should retire. But Harlan was hanging on solely because he'd cornered the defense market in Moonshine Hollow and was part of the good ol' boys club who arranged plea bargains around the bar at Opossum's Lodge.

Zoey let out a deep breath. She might not be a lawyer according to the Tennessee bar, but that didn't mean she couldn't help her friend out by proving Maribelle's innocence. If she left Maribelle's case up to Harlan, her best friend would be spending the rest of her life in prison.

10

"WELL, I'm sorry. It's not like I did it on purpose," Agnes said defensively.

Zoey tilted her head to the side as her brows furrowed in confusion.

"I told you, it was an accident," Agnes huffed.

Zoey leaned over to Vilma, not taking her eyes off Agnes on hands and knees in her living room nose to nose with a beautiful black cat. "Why is Agnes talking to a cat?"

The cat's coat was dark as night and shiny. The cat turned to look at her and Zoey almost gasped. Bright teal eyes looked her over before dismissing her and focusing back on Agnes.

"That's not a cat," Vilma whispered back.

Zoey took in the twitch of the tail that showed the annoyance of the animal. "No, I'm pretty sure that's a cat."

Vilma shook her head nervously. "Quiet, she can hear you. That's Grand Mistress Lauren. She's the head of the Claritase."

"Knock it off," Zoey laughed. The cat's head turned and her eyes narrowed. The teal color intensified and Zoey felt power surround her, then suddenly she heard a voice in her head.

"Mistress Zoey. I've heard about your little accident." The black cat approached her and Zoey felt as if someone were trying to shuffle through her brain. "Ah, I see you're smart enough to be afraid of your powers. I don't like it, but Agnes and Vilma have convinced me that they can train you instead of them taking your powers from you."

"They've done a great job so far," Zoey said, slipping her hand into Vilma's for support. "And I'd really prefer not to die."

Grand Mistress Lauren sniffed as if it were a chuckle. "I've known Vilma and Agnes for thousands of years. Trouble is what they are. However, they do know their magic. I'll allow you both to train her, but as quickly as possible. The reason I am here is to warn you. There has been a shift—black magic. I feel it pressing in on the town. It's swirling around the town searching for us."

"I've felt it," Zoey said softly. "Fear so overwhelming I kind of, um, exploded."

Grand Mistress Lauren rolled her bright teal eyes. "The future of our kind is dependent on someone who explodes out of fear. How is she going to defeat the Tenebris?"

Zoey felt her powers begin to freak out inside her. Her? It was up to her to defeat the Tenebris? "I'm sorry, I must have heard you incorrectly."

Grand Mistress Lauren shook her head. "You heard me right. The Tenebris have been gathering power by slowly killing off our healers. The man whose powers you have taken was one of their best hunters. He has taken the lives of many of our sisters. Now you've inherited all of their powers *and* his. Somehow they've been activated." The cat looked her over skeptically.

"Do you think it's the prophecy?" Agnes asked.

The cat's head nodded. "It's too early to say for sure, but it's possible."

"What prophecy?" Zoey asked looking between them.

"It's not important yet. Either way, it's time for the Claritase to come out of hiding. We will provide a distraction to spare you some time to train, but we can only hold them off for so long. May the Goddess protect us all."

With a flick of her tail, the elegant cat disappeared.

Zoey blinked at where Grand Mistress Lauren had been sitting. "I'm so confused," she muttered as if this was all a dream.

"Grand Mistress Lauren has been the head of the Claritase since Alexander killed our former Mistress, Helena, under the guise of a white flag. Lauren's a powerful witch, but during a battle with the Tenebris she had shapeshifted to try to sneak up on Alexander and was caught, her powers were pulled from her before some of our sisters could get to her. They were able to, as you say, *poof* away, but from then on Grand Mistress Lauren didn't have enough power to transform back to her human form. And only Grand Mistresses, Grand Masters, or true loves can give you power. Until then, she's a cat, but a powerful one. But for now, the most important thing is to keep you hidden while you learn all you can. Whatever you do, don't draw attention to yourself." Agnes let out a huff and for the first time seemed nervous. And that scared Zoey more than any talking cat ever could.

~

"I'll have her plead guilty. She'll be sentenced to twenty years and be out in twelve."

Zoey blinked, absolutely dumfounded, at the attorney's statement. Harlan Weaver was the laziest attorney she'd ever met. "But Maribelle is innocent! The prosecutor has no evidence that she killed Tim."

"Now little lady, don't get yourself all worked up. I have a deal with the judge and the prosecutor. They all said they'll accept the plea. All nice and neat and Maribelle will be out of jail before you know it," Harlan said dismissively.

Zoey felt the powers inside her swirling, and she was tempted to let them flow. Her fingers itched with heat, but she took a deep breath to calm them. "Will you please give me a week to look into the case? If I can prove Maribelle is innocent, your job will be even easier."

Harlan ran a hand over his trimmed gray beard. "Hmm, you may have a point. And the judge was really wanting to go to the lake soon." Zoey kept quiet. She had learned there were times to argue and times to let men think they were coming up with a plan all on their own. "Yes, I think I'll mention it to the judge when I see him at the Opossums tonight. He'll love that I was able to clear his docket for him before his lake trip."

Zoey tried not to roll her eyes. Sure, *he'll* find the evidence to clear Maribelle before the judge's lake trip. But if it meant Maribelle was cleared, she'd happily let Harlan take the credit. And if all else failed, Zoey would hire an attorney from Chattanooga or Knoxville to represent Maribelle and Dale.

WITH THE DEAL MADE, Zoey had one week to prove her best friend's innocence and learn how to not only control, but also use, her accidental witch powers. She took a deep breath. And she'd thought being the attorney for Scott

Westerfield was stressful. Wading into the fray of escorts battling strippers over a drugged out, naked Scott was nothing compared to the stress Zoey was feeling to save Agnes, Vilma, and now Maribelle and Dale. Zoey wanted to give into the fear, but then who would save her friends? So Zoey shook off the pessimism and pulled up her big girl panties. She didn't let people get the best of her in negotiations, and she wasn't going to let some evil witches and a lazy legal system get her now.

With renewed determination, Zoey's next stop was the jail. Luke sat behind his desk and at least looked pained when he saw her walking toward him. "I want to see Dale and Maribelle."

"You're not their attorney," Luke said on a sigh.

"I'm not here as their attorney, but as their private investigator. I have one week to present evidence of their innocence or Harlan is going to try to lock them up under a plea deal you know is total bull." Zoey crossed her arms over her chest and stared down at Luke.

"Then you mean *we* have a week. I don't think they did it either, and at least they're smart enough to try to find a new attorney. They've been making calls to Knoxville this morning." Luke stood up and grabbed a set of keys. "They're in the same cell. It'll give them a taste of marriage."

Zoey followed Luke through a metal door with a small square window in it to a row of cells. Well, three cells anyway. That's all there were in Moonshine Hollow. The first cell was utilized as a drunk tank. The empty second cell had a divider up in it so you couldn't see the third cell from the first cell. When she walked past the divider she saw why. Since there were no women-only cells and in order to keep Maribelle here, they had to give her privacy.

"Thank you," Zoey said softly. This wasn't something Sheriff Weller would ever think of.

"You're welcome. I'm hopeful it'll just be for a short duration, and I thought they'd be more comfortable together than having to send Maribelle to another county."

"Zoey!" Maribelle cried the second she saw her. Maribelle rushed to the door and reached through the bars. Zoey clasped her hand as Luke opened the door for them.

"I'll leave the door open at the end of the hall. Just shout when you're ready for me to let you out," Luke said, his voice heavy with regret.

Zoey hurried in and embraced Maribelle as Dale stood tall behind her with a comforting hand on her shoulder. They would get through this. Zoey swore to it as the cell door clanged shut.

"Did you hear about Harlan?" Zoey asked as she shared the horrid plea deal with them.

"We have to get a new attorney," Dale said, sounding more like a curse. "He's going to put us in jail for something we didn't do. We've left messages with a couple this morning but haven't heard back yet."

"I agree you need someone else," Zoey told them. "I did get him to give me a week to prove you didn't kill Tim. Luke said he'd help me. But if I can't prove your innocence, I'll make sure you have a new attorney by the end of the week. Tomorrow, when you go in for your bail hearing, make sure you both plead not guilty before Harlan has a chance to open his mouth."

Dale and Maribelle nodded. "Thank you, Zoey," they said with a look of hope. She only hoped she could do more to help them.

. . .

ZOEY WALKED out of the sheriff's office and stopped when she heard her name called from across the street. When Zoey looked up she saw Missy standing at the door to the Mountaineers' club.

"Yoo-hoo, Zoey!" Missy waved a ring-less hand.

Zoey crossed the street and smiled. She liked Missy. Missy was all that was southern charm and manners. She volunteered for everything, sent get well baskets when people were sick, waved to every car that drove down the street, and had a glass of sweet tea at the ready in case someone stopped by her Pawpaw's house to sit a spell.

"Hi Missy. How are you?" Zoey asked as she stepped onto the sidewalk. Some of the members of the club smiled at them as they walked inside.

"Oh, as well as can be expected. I can't believe Maribelle and Dale murdered Tim. I just had to see how she is doing. My heart is breaking for them. They are so in love, and now they'll have to get married in prison," Missy said as she wrung her hands.

"That's very nice of you to worry, Missy, but they didn't kill Tim."

"Like hell they didn't," came Wayne's hard voice from behind her. "It's all over town. They're going to take a plea deal and spend years in prison for it."

Zoey watched Wayne walk around her and slip his arm over Missy's shoulder. "I've talked to Harlan, and he said it's as good as done."

"I'll bring them a pie," Missy said to no one in particular. "Can they have pie in prison?"

"They aren't pleading guilty, Wayne. They are innocent. Why are you wearing that jacket? Aren't you hot?" Zoey asked as calmly as she could. Wayne was so thick-headed.

Wayne bristled as he looked down at the camouflaged

jacket he had zipped up to his neck and a matching hat pulled low over his eyes. "I just got back from duck hunting with Justin. And that's not what I heard, Miss High and Mighty. And I'm in the know around here. Aren't I babe?" he asked Missy.

"Oh, you sure are. Wayne knows everything." Missy bobbed her head and looked lovingly up at Wayne.

Wayne puffed up. "I'm glad *someone* appreciates me." Missy smiled up at him and Zoey rolled her eyes.

"Hey, baby."

Zoey groaned out loud. She didn't mean to, but she wasn't in the mood for Justin right now. "Hi Justin," Zoey forced out as the man wearing a matching outfit to Wayne stopped next to her.

Justin held out a new shotgun. "It's a beauty, ain't it? I got it last night and Wayne and I went out this morning so I could break it in. Got three ducks with it. How about some dinner tonight?" Why couldn't Justin be standoffish again?

"I'm sorry, but I'm busy all week with Agnes and Vilma. I promised I'd help them with a project. But fresh duck sounds delicious. Enjoy." There. Zoey was rather pleased with herself. She'd been nice when she wanted to scream that she didn't have time to worry about a date when the balance of good and evil rested on her burning fingertips.

"Come on, babe. The Mountaineers' meeting is starting soon. We have to replace Dale as president and Maribelle as secretary." Wayne leaned forward, getting closer to Zoey and winked.

"Wayne's running for president and I'm running for secretary. We'll be the new power couple of the town." Missy giggled as Wayne used his hand at the small of her back to turn her and push her inside.

"You could have had all this," Wayne gloated. Oh yeah,

Zoey was torn up over it. But now there were far more important things to spend her time on than Wayne's ego. She needed to prove Maribelle's and Dale's innocence and learn a millennium or two of witchcraft. What could go wrong?

11

"BAIL IS SET at two hundred thousand dollars each." The judge banged his gavel as Maribelle and Dale looked crestfallen.

They looked over their shoulders at her and Zoey smiled encouragingly. Maybe their parents would use their houses for collateral, but she doubted they could afford it. At the worst, they would be in jail another week if bail couldn't be raised. The judge was holding a preliminary hearing next week before he left for vacation. It would be there that Zoey could push for dismissal.

"We don't have the money," Maribelle sniffed between silent tears.

"It's okay. One week. You all can do it. It'll be like a honeymoon," Zoey tried to say positively. The look Maribelle gave her told her she'd failed in her attempt to cheer up her friend. Sheriff Weller grabbed them both by the arm and walked them out of the courthouse.

"One week, Miss Mathers," Harlan threatened as he walked by her, whistling.

Luke came to stand by her. "The State Police have the autopsy in. You didn't get this from me."

Zoey looked down and took the folder he handed her. She shoved it into her purse. "Any luck on the email?"

"We tracked it to one of the computers at Mountaineers, but that could be anyone."

Zoey sighed. The prosecutor would say that was evidence it was Dale and Maribelle. "Has the provider gotten back to you with the account holder's name?"

"Not yet," Luke told her as they walked outside.

"What time was it sent?" Zoey asked.

"Eight minutes past two in the morning."

Zoey looked around the courthouse and down the street. "I'm guessing no surveillance cameras?"

Luke just looked at her.

"Yeah, yeah, Moonshine Hollow has no crime so why would they need cameras?" Zoey asked sarcastically. "Too bad you have a crime to solve and no cameras." She took a deep breath. "So all I have to do is find out who was here at that time and then we have our suspect." Yeah, that was a plan. She could do that. Zoey psyched herself up. She'd watched an old episode of *Murder, She Wrote* last night and had *Perry Mason* set to record on her DVR. She was all over this amateur sleuthing.

"Check out the autopsy," Luke said as they stood by themselves at the corner of the courthouse.

Zoey opened the file and scanned. Tim had been strangled, but it was the broken neck that had killed him. Time of death was one fifty in the morning. "So the killer killed Tim at one fifty, then walked to the club, broke in, and sent the email. The timeline matches."

Luke nodded. "I already checked out Mountaineers this morning. The door was not broken into. There were no scrapes around the lock, and Bethany swore she locked the doors before leaving for the park that night. Read the rest."

Zoey looked back at the report. Self-defense wounds. Skin was found under Tim's nails. "The suspect will have scratches on them, scrape marks. Did you take pictures of Dale and Maribelle when they were booked?"

"Sure did."

"And?" Zoey pushed about to run out of patience.

"Not a single scrape on them. No bruising, no scrapes, no cuts. Nothing."

Zoey felt her heart speed up. "We have the evidence to clear them."

"You know the judge will want more," Luke told her, trying to rein in her excitement.

"Now we have a time of death. Let's get Maribelle and Dale's alibi, because I know they weren't out killing Tim."

"They were together. No other witnesses. They went to Maribelle's house after the Moonshine of the Year announcement," Luke said, putting his hands in the pockets of his jeans. So that wasn't going to help Maribelle and Dale.

"Okay." Zoey took a deep breath and refocused. "Get DNA samples from them both, and compare it to the skin under Tim's nails. In the meantime, I need to think of a way to get the Mountaineers all in one place so we can see if anyone has any bruises or scrapes."

⁓

"No! Do it again," Agnes huffed.

Zoey looked sadly at Chance sitting in front of her. His dark brown eyes blinked up at her. His white tipped black tail thumped on the floor as if she hadn't just zapped him with magic.

"I'm so sorry," Zoey apologized before feeling the power build inside her. She visualized the bedroom in Agnes and Vilma's house and wiggled her fingers. *Poof*, the puppy disappeared.

"I did it!" Zoey said in wonder as Vilma opened the bedroom door and Chance ran out.

"Very good. I think that's it for tonight. I heard you are hosting a Mountaineer Muffin day tomorrow," Vilma said as they walked back into the living room. "Any reason you suddenly are giving free muffins to the Mountaineers tomorrow?"

"You can't say a word or I'll hit you with the silencing spell you taught me." Zoey stared them down. When they didn't look intimidated she rolled her eyes and continued. "I read Tim's autopsy. He scratched his attacker, *hard*. The attacker used the Mountaineers' computer at two in the morning to send the recipe to Ronald Stone asking for a million dollars for the rest of the recipes."

"Well, we can help with that," Agnes said, taking a seat on the floral couch.

"Help? I didn't ask for—"

Vilma waved her off. "We'll be sneaky. No one will know what we are looking for."

Great. Now she's going to have two nosy senior witches to look after as well as trying to find the killer, free her friends, and save the witch world. What else could possibly be added to pile?

∼

ZOEY CLOSED her eyes and took in the sounds and smells of her kitchen. It was four in the morning. She'd only had four hours of sleep thanks to her late night witch lessons.

Exhaustion was days ago. Now she was running solely on coffee.

She took a deep breath and inhaled the rich scent of the coffee, along with the rolling warmth of the ovens heating to life and the smell of the ingredients sitting on the prep table. The sounds of Chance snoring in his bed and crickets from the open kitchen door were music to her. Zoey opened her eyes and smiled. This made her happy. It made her soul sing, and she felt the magic inside her bubbling with excitement. All of which told her exactly what she needed to hear—Moonshine Hollow and Zoey's Sweet Treats was where she belonged all along.

Hours later she had muffins, scones, and chocolate-filled croissants lining the tables in the kitchen and filling the display case out front. Zoey wiped the flour from her hands and dusted off her apron. She went and opened the front door at seven and found Vilma and Agnes waiting.

"About time. We were about to pop into the kitchen. But we didn't risk it since you tend to explode when you get scared," Agnes said dryly.

"I'll start the coffee," Vilma called out as she brushed past Zoey and headed for the coffee on the counter.

"I just have a basket of muffins I want to bring out front before people get here," Zoey called as she headed into the back. Suddenly her spine stiffened. Her powers surged. She felt it. Evil was near.

"Deep breaths." A voice pushed through her fear. "Focus on the fear. Don't run from it. See the fear and pull it to you. Form it into a tight ball in the pit of your stomach. See the power in the fear then you can control it."

Zoey's eyes were unseeing as the voice spoke to her. Her gaze was internal as she pulled the fear from her fingertips, up her arms, into her stomach where it met with the fear from her toes that had traveled up her legs. There, in her stomach, was a glowing ball of black energy.

"That's right. Now you control it. Send it to your hand and hold the power and energy of fear in your hand," the voice instructed.

Zoey pictured the ball moving up to her arm then down to her hand. When she blinked back to reality, she saw a ball of black light burning like a hunk of coal in her hand. Agnes and Vilma stood absolutely still at the entrance to the kitchen staring in wonder.

"That is how you control a weapon such as fear, you can embrace it."

Neither Agnes's nor Vilma's mouths moved. Zoey was confused until she felt something brush her leg. She looked down and found Grand Mistress Lauren's teal eyes looking up at her.

"Wow." Zoey felt a shift inside her. It was as if the magic knew she had taken control. "Now what do I do with it?"

"Just let it go," Grand Mistress Lauren told her.

Zoey looked at the mystical ball floating in the palm of her hand. She widened her fingers and commanded the fear to leave. In slow wisps of energy, the ball dissolved into the air as if a candle had been blown out.

Grand Mistress Lauren was gone when Zoey looked down.

The bell over the door rang as Zoey, Agnes, and Vilma headed out front.

"Oh my," Zoey heard the old ladies gasp.

"What is it?" Zoey asked as she came out front and stopped dead in her tracks. There, in her shop, stood six foot five inches of muscle and leather.

"Slade?" Zoey asked in surprise.

"How you doing, sweetness?"

Zoey felt the magic dancing in her blood as her face flushed. Agnes's and Vilma's heads kept going back and forth between Zoey and Slade as if watching a tennis match.

Zoey took in the tight black shirt stretched over his massive chest down to his black leather motorcycle pants and black boots. When her eyes made it back up to his face, he winked at her, causing Agnes and Vilma to gasp again. It could be from his glacial pale blue eyes or it could be that they saw what Zoey just had—a tattoo on his neck of black swords connecting to make a circle with a drop of red blood in the center. The same tattoo that had been on the man who Zoey had accidently consumed the powers from.

"Ladies," his deep voice rumbled as he looked over at Agnes and Vilma.

A wave of energy flew past Zoey heading straight for Agnes and Vilma. Zoey couldn't see it, but she felt it. She leapt in front of her friends and the energy crashed into her. Zoey plastered a smile on her face, ignoring the power surge that had just slammed into her as she put up a mental shield.

"What on earth are you doing here? I never thought I would see you again. Agnes, Vilma, this is Slade. I met him in California. Actually," Zoey said with a cock of her head, "he said it was fate I would end up here."

His eyebrows temporarily creased in confusion before clearing so fast she almost missed it. The power surged backed off. "I couldn't stop thinking of what happened to you. You sure know how to make an impression. I thought I'd see how you were doing. I've taken some time off and am traveling cross country on the bike. It was always a dream of mine to tour the country."

Zoey gave him a "yeah, right" look, and it appeared

Slade thought about grinning. "Okay," he said calmly as he held up his hands. "I'm also here on work."

Agnes looked over Zoey's shoulder and let out a whistle. "Is that bike yours?"

"Yes, ma'am," Slade answered as Zoey looked out the window. That was a sexy bike and the image of Slade on it . . . whew, she suddenly felt very hot.

"Care to take some old ladies for a ride?" Vilma asked as the first Mountaineer opened the door.

"Hey Justin," Zoey smiled as she cringed. A war was being waged inside her. Was Slade dangerous? Was he part of the Tenebris? It was too weird that she felt the fear and then he came in, right? He had the same tattoo as the guy Vilma zapped. Plus she'd felt the energy. It was the same energy Grand Mistress Lauren used to get into her mind. What was going on?

Slade turned and Justin froze in surprise. "Oh, you must be new here. Welcome to Moonshine Hollow."

"Thanks," Slade said, crossing his arms over his massive chest and looking at Justin through narrowed eyes.

The door opened again as Missy and Wayne came in. Wayne looked at Slade and frowned. He walked over with a cocky swagger. "Some goth show in town?"

Zoey sent a panicked look to Agnes and Vilma. They didn't need to say anything. They knew Slade was trouble. Too bad he was the kind of trouble Zoey and every other red blooded female wished would show up at their door. Even Missy was staring at him with her mouth open as if she was picturing him naked.

Slade turned and gave Zoey a wink. Zoey slammed her mental walls closed and turned to Wayne. "Wayne, what can I get you and Missy?" She said Missy's name loudly to disrupt Missy's drooling over Slade and the trouble that could erupt. Before Wayne could answer, the door opened and more men and women streamed in chatting animatedly. Zoey, Agnes, and Vilma stared in horror.

"They're all wearing camouflage jackets and hats," Zoey whispered in panic. The jackets zipped up to their chins and the ball caps sat low on their foreheads. What the heck?

12

"I CAN FIX one of those problems," Vilma muttered as she walked up to Justin in the front of the line and smacked the hat off his head. "Where are all y'all's manners? You don't wear hats inside a restaurant!"

"Sorry ma'am," came the collective grumbling as everyone pulled off their hats. Justin had a black eye that had been hidden under his hat and Vilma latched herself onto him, trying to peer down his jacket and examining his face.

"Ma'am?" Justin asked with confusion.

"Just seeing if you got any more injuries besides that black eye. What happened to you?" Vilma stepped back and handed him a muffin.

"My two year old nephew head butted me. I'm glad nothing's broken. It hurt like the devil, but he laughed his head off at Uncle Justin rolling on the floor in pain."

Agnes started mingling as Luke came in. He stopped suddenly in shock from all the camo or the image of Slade standing in the middle of it all, Zoey didn't know which.

"What's going on?" Slade asked, tilting his head down toward her.

"The camo? I have no idea?" Zoey responded absently as her eyes roamed from person to person.

"Oh." Missy giggled from where she still hadn't moved from Slade's side. "I bet we look strange. It's the annual Mountaineers duck hunt. We're a club, would you like to join me . . . I mean us?"

Slade didn't respond, instead he simply looked at Missy and gave a small smile. Missy blinked and turned bright red before Wayne grabbed her hand and dragged her up to Vilma.

"My, that's a nasty bruise to the side of your head," Vilma said to Wayne, drawing Zoey's attention.

"Spill it," Slade said so low it was more of a rumble.

Zoey stood on her tiptoes as Slade bent down. "There was a murder and two innocent people are in jail. The murderer was scratched and bruised by the victim."

Slade didn't respond, he just straightened up and scanned the crowd as Luke pushed his way through. He narrowed his eyes at Slade and came to stand on Zoey's other's side.

"I'm Deputy Sheriff Luke Tanner. Who are you?" Luke asked Slade pointedly.

"Slade. Nice to meet you, Deputy." Slade didn't look as if it were nice to meet Luke. In fact, he looked annoyed.

"Are you the guy who has been seen driving a motorcycle around town?"

"The one you told me about? The one you were looking for?" Zoey whispered to Luke. Luke gave a curt nod.

"When did you get to town?" Luke asked, although it sounded more like a demand to Zoey.

"A little bit ago," Slade calmly replied.

"Where are you staying?" Luke asked in full interrogation mode.

"A cabin in the woods that I rented online."

"Why are you here?" Zoey shifted back and forth as she felt herself begin to sweat. She realized she was nervous for Slade. Or was she really hot?

"Work. And I like staying in the cabin because it's quiet. I enjoy nature, and it's quite relaxing out there," Slade told him. "Excuse me."

Slade stepped back and walked out the front door without saying a word. Zoey watched with surprise as he strode around the building and out of sight.

"Well, this certainly worked and backfired all at the same time," Luke said. "The motorcycle suspect I've been looking for is right here . . . or he was. And we need to identify the suspect with bruised arms, which I noticed Slade didn't have. But everyone is covered in hunting gear."

"There has to be a way to get them to roll up their sleeves," Zoey muttered to herself.

"So, who is Slade to you?" Luke asked as his eyes scanned the crowd.

"Someone I met in California."

"Boyfriend?" Luke asked a little more casually than Zoey would have liked. He didn't sound jealous at all. In fact, she might even describe it as hopeful. Not that Zoey was trying to make Luke jealous, but a little jealousy could go a long way stroking a girl's ego.

"Nope." Zoey responded equally as calm. "Is it getting hot in here or is it just me?" Zoey looked back at the kitchen and saw a figure in black moving about through the small glass windows in the doors. What was Slade doing in the kitchen?

"It's blazing hot. I guess it's all these people," Luke said as sweat began to dot his brow. Women began to fan themselves with their caps and men began to take off their jackets.

Zoey's eyes shot back to the kitchen, but Slade was gone. She stepped back against the wall and felt the hot air streaming from the vent. Slade had turned the heat up and now people were sweating and removing their coats.

Zoey felt Slade slip back into the shop as she took her basket of muffins and began going person to person handing them out, slowly making her way to the front of the line. Justin shook out of his coat and Zoey held her breath until she saw his neck and arms—not a scratch.

"Let me get more muffins," Zoey smiled as she moved behind the counter. Vilma traded places with her, slowly mingling down the long line offering them hot coffee as she looked at arms and necks. Slade stood unmoving as the tide of people parted around him.

Luke stepped into line, and while he appeared relaxed, Zoey saw his eyes taking in every bare arm, every nick, scratch, and bruise as the line slowly moved. Agnes and Vilma chatted everyone up, keeping them in the long slow line while Zoey moved as slow as possible, allowing the heat to become almost unbearable.

Person after person reached out for their free muffins and coffee as they all shed their coats. Denny reached for his muffin and Zoey gasped. "Oh dear, what happened to your arm?"

There, running the length of his forearm were four scratches. They didn't appear to be big enough to be from Tim though. Denny took the muffin and looked down at his arm. "Oh. Some stray cat did this. Nancy saw this black cat strutting down the street. It had teal eyes and Nancy was in love. Made me go get it so she could adopt it."

"Teal eyes?" Zoey asked as casually as she could.

"Yeah, you've seen it?" When Zoey nodded Denny continued. "Lots of strays around town recently. Last night I saw a cat and a hawk sitting side by side on the fence. Never seen the likes of it in my life."

Denny shook his shaggy blond head and Zoey tried not to smile. Denny was under a spell all right, his new wife's. He'd do anything for her. Zoey had a feeling that the animals Denny was talking about weren't really strays though. Her new sisters had arrived.

"I reached for the cat and the cat had other ideas. Scraped me to ribbons. Well, thanks for the muffin. Can I get one for Nancy? She's outside, trying to catch another cat that's strolling down the sidewalk."

Zoey handed a second muffin over, trying not to laugh. She could imagine Grand Mistress Lauren being a little peeved at someone trying to pick her up.

Agnes made her way behind the counter and nudged Zoey, who was handing a muffin to another perfectly tanned and slightly hairy man without a single scratch to be seen before another young woman came up to get her free muffin.

"Excuse me, I need to refill the case." Zoey smiled at Mildred and hurried to the back. Bless her poor heart for being named after her dead great-grandmother. "What is it?" Zoey asked Agnes.

"Everyone has taken off their coats except one. Strange, isn't it?"

Zoey grabbed a tray and headed back to the slowly thinning group. She let her eyes scan the line before going back to grab the last tray.

"How do we get the coat off?"

"Leave that up to me, dearie." Agnes grabbed the pot of

fresh brewed coffee and headed out with a look of pure determination on her face. Oh no. This wasn't going to go well.

Zoey rushed after her. "Agnes," she whispered harshly but it was too late. For someone thousands of years old, the woman could move very quickly. Zoey watched as if it was all happening in slow motion. Agnes pushed through to the line, tripped over an invisible object, and dumped the entire pot of steaming hot coffee on the last person wearing a jacket.

"Yeow!!!" Wayne leapt back, knocking Missy into Luke, sending the two tumbling to the ground, as he ripped the scalding hot jacket from his body.

"Oh my gosh! I'm so sorry," Zoey called as she hurried to him. The rest of the line was moving out of the way as Wayne filled the small shop with curses.

It wasn't the cursing that got Zoey's attention though. It was the numerous deep scrape marks on Wayne's arm that looked as if Tim had raked his nails frantically against Wayne's arm in an attempt to escape a chokehold.

Wayne stopped cussing when he saw Zoey's eyes on his arm. He looked behind him and saw Missy on top of Luke, but there was no mistaking Luke's knowing look. Wayne shot his hand out and dragged Zoey to him. His forearm slid around her neck from behind as Zoey felt the power inside her surge. If she didn't get control of herself, she'd explode again, taking out who knew how many people and letting Slade know she was the witch he was looking for. Focus on the fear, Grand Mistress Lauren had told her. Don't run from it.

Luke shoved a screaming Missy from him as Wayne thrust a hunting knife against Zoey's side. Zoey gasped as the sharp tip dug into her skin.

"Nobody move," Wayne said clearly as the shop that had been in chaos froze. Most people had run outside and were now looking in through the windows. Some of them were reaching in their trucks for their gun racks and the few left inside were frozen in disbelief in the middle of her shop.

"Put it down, Luke," Wayne warned as Luke reached for his gun.

Luke looked back and forth between Wayne and Zoey and finally decided to set the gun down. "Why'd you do it, Wayne?" Luke asked as he motioned for Missy to stop her screeching and slowly stood up.

Zoey sucked in a breath. It wasn't the knife slowly piercing her skin above her rib that was the problem. It was the rush of magic she felt flowing around the room. Wave after wave of it hit her even as Agnes, Vilma, and Slade showed no indication of feeling it. Instead, Agnes and Vilma looked as if they were about to jump into the fray. Luke looked as if he were going to talk Wayne down. And Slade . . . well, he just looked pissed off. Zoey shivered at the cold waves of anger washing over him. She felt them and eyed him wearily. He looked bent on murder. The question was whose? Hers? Agnes's? Vilma's? Had he felt their power? Or was it Wayne because he was threatening her?

"How did you know?" Wayne asked instead.

"We found your skin under Tim's nails. We knew he had scratched his assailant. We also know that the email sent to Ronald Stone was sent from the Mountaineers' computer in the middle of the night. We knew it was a Mountaineer. We didn't know it was you until we saw the wounds. Why did you do it, Wayne?" Luke kept his gaze steady, but not intimidating.

"Why else? Money. Ronald is running his distillery into the ground, and I was meant for more than this dump. I was going to get that money and buy a mansion in the big city. Tim wasn't supposed to fight back. I always thought he was a wimp. I waited for him to start walking home and I surprised him in the dark. But Tim didn't give me the recipes when I asked. He punched me in the side of the head. He made me kill him since he didn't give me what I wanted. First Tim and now you. I was going to be rich, and you all ruined that!"

Zoey felt the knife point dig in farther. She gasped, her hands tightening over Wayne's forearm as she dug her nails into his skin, scraping him to release her, much like what Tim had done when Wayne stood behind him strangling the life from him. Fear shot through her. Slade swayed as if feeling it then he made a sound that wasn't quite human. A low growl emanated from him that no one else seemed to hear.

Zoey met Slade's piercing gaze when the tears of pain slipped from her green eyes. The bright blue had all but vanished, leaving only the coldest ice blue focused completely on her. They calmed her fear, even as she felt the magic screaming for release. Would she die or out herself as a witch? Right now Zoey didn't know as her mind and body waged against each other in a fight or flight response.

One thing she couldn't do was break her gaze with Slade's. At that moment, she was bound to him. He was her anchor. Slade lowered his chin slightly, and Zoey knew without a doubt what he wanted her to do. Slade may kill her later in a battle between good and evil, but right now he seemed her best chance at survival.

As Luke continued to talk, Zoey felt Agnes and Vilma moving closer. Zoey was completely focused on Slade as Missy sat on the floor crying. She saw him inching forward as she gathered the fear into a ball, just like Grand Mistress

Lauren taught her. She focused on the black ball and imagined it traveling up her stomach, down her arms, then she stopped it. She waited, feeling the energy growing, shifting, and turning restless. When Slade gave her a wink she made her move. She set the energy free as she dug her nails into Wayne's skin. The energy shot out her fingertips and right into his arm like an electric shock.

Wayne howled, his grip loosening enough for Zoey to drop to the ground. Slade vaulted himself through the air. Zoey closed her eyes and ducked as Slade's body flew over hers and into Wayne, knocking him to the ground where Agnes and Vilma pelted Wayne with muffins. If she thought that was bad, it was nothing compared to the haymaker Slade delivered, sending Wayne into unconsciousness.

Zoey let out an unsteady breath. Her body was beginning to shake as the increased energy and adrenaline mixed. Vilma and Agnes rushed to her as Luke grabbed up his gun and moved to kick the knife from Wayne's hand. Slade slowly stood from where he was straddling Wayne and turned to look at her.

"Oh my Goddess. If only he wasn't part of Tenebris. In the old days, the best way to handle the surge of energy rushing through our bodies after battle was sex," Agnes whispered as Slade bent down and grabbed Wayne's slack body with one hand and hauled him up.

"Here you go, Deputy. Where do you want me to put him?" Slade asked as Wayne dangled from his grip, giving the women a good view of Slade from behind.

"I'd say it's worth the risk," Vilma sighed.

Luke waved Denny in. "Help me take Wayne down to the jail."

"I can't believe it," Denny stuttered as Luke and Denny both slid in under Wayne's arms.

Slade released his grip, and Wayne fell forward between Denny and Luke. His head hung down and his legs dragged behind them as they angled themselves out the door. The Mountaineers stood quiet and made a path for Luke and Denny. Conversation erupted as soon as they were at the end of the block.

The group reassembled back inside. Zoey sucked in a breath and backed up. People pressed in on her and she felt panicked. Then Slade was there. He didn't say a word. He simply narrowed his eyes and held out a hand, stopping the entire group in their tracks.

"You two up to handling this while I check out Zoey's side to make sure she's not hurt?"

"You bet we are, stud muffin," Vilma said with a wink. Slade smiled and Agnes giggled. It was embarrassing, but Zoey was too out of it to care.

13

Slade escorted Zoey through the crowd and into the kitchen. Zoey let out a sigh of relief and then gave a squeak of surprise as Slade lifted her onto the prep table.

"Take off your shirt while I turn off the heat."

Zoey felt her mouth drop open. "I will not. I'm perfectly fine."

"You're bleeding," Slade stated matter-of-factly. "Besides, it's not as if I haven't seen it all ready. Remember, you gave me quite a show on that stage last time I saw you."

Zoey gasped as Slade let out a frustrated breath and reached over to rip her shirt across her belly as if he were pulling off a bandage. "You're hurt," Slade said with an undertone that made Zoey shiver. She felt the anger he felt. She felt the way he fought to control it.

Slade turned off the heat and the shop was soon filled with blissful air conditioning as he grabbed a towel and began to wet it. Zoey scrambled backward on the prep table, nervous about the deadly fire in Slade's eyes when he looked at her. But those eyes softened when he walked toward her. He let out an annoyed sigh as Zoey flinched at the pain in her side before snatching the towel and covering her midsection.

"Zoey, stop." Slade ordered, but not with the malevolence she expected. It was more in the tone of kindness.

Zoey stopped trying to cover her exposed midriff as Slade slowly took the towel from her hand. Slade began to clean the wound with gentleness she didn't know he possessed. "It needs stitches. Do you want me to summon the doctor?"

Zoey snorted. "Gosh, no. He'll just put an ice pack on it. I'll go to Knoxville."

"No need," Slade said before striding out the backdoor and disappearing once again.

"Oh my Goddess!" Agnes said, fanning herself as she and Vilma stumbled into the kitchen. "That man is hot enough I'd give him my powers for a couple of hours alone with him."

"Why is he here?" Vilma whispered, looking around as if he were about to pop back in.

"He's going to kill us. But what a way to go," Agnes said, continuing to fan herself.

"You want me to fix that, dear?" Vilma asked, rubbing her hands together. Vilma had taught Zoey the magic to heal just the other night, and if it weren't for Slade's presence, that's exactly what Zoey would have had Vilma do.

"I got it," Slade said, walking back into the kitchen holding a first aid kit. "I've sewn lots of people back together."

"Oh?" Vilma asked. "Is it because you're an overly violent person or do you have a medical degree under all that . . . leather?"

"I didn't think I was going to be getting blood on me today so I left my pleather pants in my bag. And no, I'm not a doctor," Slade said as he washed Zoey's wound with iodine. "But I am a soldier of sorts, and I've had to sew up people plenty of times. Now, this will pinch."

Zoey sucked in a startled breath as the needle went through her skin. She looked over Slade's head as he bent to work and looked at Agnes and Vilma. The humor in their eyes had disappeared upon hearing Slade's soldier announcement. Now fear filled them.

"Zoey, are you still here?" Before Zoey could answer Luke came in through the swinging doors. "You're hurt!"

"I got it, Deputy," Slade said coldly without taking his eyes or hands from her as he placed the last stitch.

"Are you hurt badly, Zoey?" Luke asked, ignoring Slade.

"No, I'm fine. But tell me what happened with Wayne." Zoey watched as Agnes's and Vilma's heads began to look back and forth between Luke and Slade while their brows creased in thought.

"He's been booked at the jail. The prosecutor got an emergency hearing with the judge for thirty minutes from now. I thought you would like to be there when the charges were dismissed against Maribelle and Dale."

"Oh, yes."

Slade bent down, his lips skimming her skin. Zoey sucked in a breath as her body flushed at the intimacy of the touch. His mouth opened, his teeth grazed her skin, and then there was a quick tug on the stitching thread.

"Ow!"

"All done," Slade said, standing upright after biting the suture off. He reached over for a bandage, and within seconds he was packing up his bag. "I'll see you around, sweetness. Ladies." Slade turned to Agnes and Vilma and headed out the back door.

"Was that a promise or a threat?" Luke asked into the silence as they all stared at the now empty outline of the door.

Zoey didn't know, but it was up to her to find out. For if tall, dark, and sexy was a threat, it was up to her to take him out. She felt it in her body—the battle for good and evil had started.

~

"ZOEY!" Maribelle cried as she ran down the courthouse steps. Dale was steps behind her. They looked tired, but relieved. "All charges have been dropped. It was Wayne—he confessed."

"She knows, dear. Zoey's the one who organized the capture. We can't thank you enough," Dale said, sliding his arm around Maribelle's waist as soon as Maribelle released Zoey from a tight hug.

"I'm so glad." Zoey laughed as her best friend fairly bounced with renewed life.

"Can I tell her, please?" Maribelle begged Dale, who smiled and gave a brief nod of his head. Maribelle squealed in return. "We're engaged! Dale asked me this morning in our cell. We'll need a re-do so we'll have a more appropriate story to tell our families and children someday."

"That's wonderful! Congratulations you two." Zoey hugged them both then stepped back as their friends and family hurried forward to welcome them back to freedom.

Zoey watched her friends become engulfed in loving embraces before turning toward her home. She wanted to get home, take off the apron hiding her torn shirt, and snuggle Chance.

She wasn't even past the courthouse before Agnes and Vilma flanked her on each side. A black cat with teal eyes sauntered by with a flick of her tail. An owl hooted in a nearby tree. Another cat sat cleaning herself across the street. A hawk cried as it flew by in the bright morning sky. Zoey closed her eyes for a brief second. She felt the sisterhood, the love, and the energy of the Claritase. Off in the distance, a motorcycle revved its engine. A man in black sat in the seat watching her before driving off.

"Now that Maribelle and Dale are safe, we need to increase our lessons. I fear we are running out of time," Vilma said as Agnes nodded her agreement.

With a flick of Vilma's hand, the hawk soared after Slade to keep an eye on the enemy from above.

"Do you think Slade is here to kill us?" Zoey asked.

"He has the mark of the Tenebris. We'd be stupid to think he's not here to hunt us. Even if his actions today were, well, unexpected. We must keep our guard up, and we must work hard to teach you several lifetimes of information in a few weeks," Agnes told her.

"Then we shouldn't waste any time," Zoey said, filled with determination.

She had always wanted to be a part of something. Zoey had wanted a family, and now she had sisters who were depending on her. Agnes and Vilma smiled as they walked side by side, flanked by Mistress Lauren and several other sisters marching alongside Zoey toward her fate. For now she felt the loving, healing energy of the sisterhood and she'd give her life to protect it.

The End

New Release Notifications for Kathleen Brooks, Sign Up Here:

https://kathleen-brooks.com/new-release-notifications

Subscribers will be the first to learn about the new Forever Bluegrass series coming soon.

~

Please visit the retailer's product page if you have enjoyed this story to leave a review. It helps me to know which characters and story lines the readers enjoy so I can make future books even better. Thank you!

Bluegrass Series

Bluegrass State of Mind

Risky Shot

Dead Heat

Bluegrass Brothers

Bluegrass Undercover

Rising Storm

Secret Santa: A Bluegrass Series Novella

Acquiring Trouble

Relentless Pursuit

Secrets Collide

Final Vow

Bluegrass Singles

All Hung Up

Bluegrass Dawn

The Perfect Gift

The Keeneston Roses

Forever Bluegrass Series

Forever Entangled

Forever Hidden

Forever Betrayed

Forever Driven

Forever Secret

Forever Surprised

Forever Concealed

Forever Devoted

Forever Hunted

Forever Guarded

Forever Notorious

Forever Ventured (coming later in 2019)

<u>*Shadows Landing Series*</u>

Saving Shadows

Sunken Shadows (coming May 14, 2019)

Lasting Shadows (coming later in 2019)

<u>Women of Power Series</u>

Chosen for Power

Built for Power

Fashioned for Power

Destined for Power

<u>*Web of Lies Series*</u>

Whispered Lies

Rogue Lies

Shattered Lies

<u>*Moonshine Hollow Series*</u>

Moonshine & Murder

Moonshine & Malice (coming March 26, 2019)

Moonshine & Mayhem (coming April 16, 2019)

ABOUT THE AUTHOR

Kathleen Brooks is a New York Times, Wall Street Journal, and USA Today bestselling author. Kathleen's stories are romantic suspense featuring strong female heroines, humor, and happily-ever-afters. Her Bluegrass Series and follow-up Bluegrass Brothers Series feature small town charm with quirky characters that have captured the hearts of readers around the world.

Kathleen is an animal lover who supports rescue organizations and other non-profit organizations such as Friends and Vets Helping Pets whose goals are to protect and save our four-legged family members.

Email Notice of New Releases

https://kathleen-brooks.com/new-release-notifications

Kathleen's Website
www.kathleen-brooks.com
Facebook Page
www.facebook.com/KathleenBrooksAuthor
Twitter
www.twitter.com/BluegrassBrooks
Goodreads
www.goodreads.com

Made in United States
North Haven, CT
09 November 2022

26493521R00071